viva vermont!

OTHER BOOKS BY MELODY CARLSON:

Carter House Girls series

Mixed Bags (Book One)
Stealing Bradford (Book Two)

Girls of 622 Harbor View series

Project: Girl Power (Book One)
Project: Mystery Bus (Book Two)
Project: Rescue Chelsea (Book Three)
Project: Take Charge (Book Four)
Project: Raising Faith (Book Five)
Project: Run Away (Book Six)
Project: Ski Trip (Book Seven)
Project: Secret Admirer (Book Eight)

Books for Teens

The Secret Life of Samantha McGregor series
Diary of a Teenage Girl series
TrueColors series
Notes from a Spinning Planet series
Degrees series
Piercing Proverbs
By Design series

Women's Fiction

These Boots Weren't Made for Walking
On This Day
An Irish Christmas
The Christmas Bus
Crystal Lies
Finding Alice
Three Days

Grace Chapel Inn Series including

Hidden History
Ready to Wed
Back Home Again

carter house girls

viva vermont!

melody carlson

ZONDERVAN®

ZONDERVAN.com/
AUTHORTRACKER
follow your favorite authors

ZONDERVAN®

Viva Vermont!
Copyright © 2008 by Melody Carlson

Requests for information should be addressed to:

Zondervan, *Grand Rapids, Michigan 49530*

Library of Congress Cataloging-in-Publication Data: Applied for
ISBN 978-0-310-71491-0

Interior design by Christine Orejuela-Winkelman

Printed in the United States of America

08 09 10 11 12 13 14 • 20 19 18 17 16 15 14 13 12 11 10 9 8 7 6 5 4 3 2 1

viva vermont!

DJ STILL FELT LIKE CINDERELLA the next morning—Cinderella after the magic was gone, that is. Not that she wasn't still pumped about last night. Who would've thought that she, of all people, would be crowned homecoming queen? But now it was Saturday morning, and her grandmother was droning on and on about today's BIG fashion show, like she thought they were walking a runway in Paris instead of Crescent Cove, Connecticut.

"And I expect my girls to behave themselves as ladies," Grandmother said as the six girls poked at their breakfast of granola, fresh fruit, and plain yogurt. For no explainable reason, DJ was craving bacon, eggs, and pancakes slathered in butter and syrup. Like that was going to happen.

"You will be representing Carter House ... and me," continued Grandmother. "And this fashion show is your debut in the community. I expect all of you to put your very best foot forward."

"That would be my right foot." DJ held up her cane and frowned down at her large walking cast. "Do I still have to do this, Grandmother? My leg is really aching today."

"That's because you were such a show-off last night." Eliza's tone was teasing, but DJ sensed a hard glint in her pretty blue eyes.

"You're just jealous," said Taylor as she refilled her coffee cup.

"I most certainly am not," said Eliza, her chin held high. "I couldn't be happier for DJ. I thought it was just the sweetest thing ever seeing her limping forward with her cute little cane to receive the crown. Even my parents were glad for her."

Casey made a snorting laugh of disbelief, and Grandmother gave her a stern look. "Sorry," said Casey sarcastically. "But I happened to have been sitting directly behind Eliza's parents last night, and I heard her mother gasp when they announced DJ's name over the loudspeaker."

Eliza blinked. "Well, that's only because she was surprised."

Grandmother cleared her throat. "We were all rather surprised to see Desiree crowned queen last night." Then she actually smiled at DJ, in a way that made DJ wonder if Grandmother had been just a little bit pleased.

"I wasn't surprised," said Rhiannon. "It was the buzz at school yesterday."

"The buzz?" Eliza frowned. "Like who even uses that word anymore?"

Rhiannon just shrugged, and Casey looked like she wanted to say something that would probably get her excused from the table. Instead, Grandmother continued her monologue about the fashion show.

"Well, I'm sure you must all be ready to put the homecoming queen competition behind you now, girls. We need to focus on today's big event. I want you all to be at your very best." She pointed a finger at DJ. "And, yes, Desiree, I certainly do expect you to participate today. After all, this show is part of

8

the Crescent Cove Homecoming weekend. The alumni would certainly appreciate seeing this year's reigning queen amongst the models. Take some pain medication if you need to. Besides, you only have one outfit to show, how hard can that be? Really, I don't think it's too much to expect you to contribute your best effort. This is, after all, for a very good cause."

"What very good cause?" asked DJ.

Grandmother frowned. "Well, I don't recall offhand, but I do know it's something worthwhile." She glanced up at the clock on the sideboard. "And we need to be at Keller Tavern by eleven."

"Keller Tavern?" questioned Casey. "Will they be serving beer?"

Grandmother gave Casey a withering look. "No. For your information, Keller Tavern is a historic inn that dates back more than two hundred years, and it is merely the finest restaurant in this part of Connecticut."

"So, no beer then ..." Taylor exchanged a smirk with Casey, and DJ wondered if those two were actually starting to get along again.

"Anyway," said Grandmother loudly, "I'm sure you girls will want to spend plenty of time in preparation. Makeup, nails, hair ... all must be absolute perfection."

"Why nails?" asked DJ as she peered at her hands. "I mean, who's going to see our nails?"

"I'm sure that I've already mentioned that I expect some very important fashion people to be in attendance at this event." Grandmother stood stiffly. She was clearly getting impatient. "And I want you girls to look divine." She smiled directly at Taylor and Eliza now. "You just never know. Some of you girls may be scouted for some other important fashion projects. You must always be ready for the unexpected." Grandmother smiled and patted her silver hair.

"And if you'll excuse me, I want to be sure that I am looking my best as well." With narrow eyes, she peered at all of them. "So, do not be late, girls. I expect to see you all at Keller Tavern at eleven sharp. Until then."

"*Until then*," said DJ in an affected voice, but only after Grandmother was out of earshot.

"So, you guys aren't actually taking this seriously?" asked Casey. She seemed to be directing this to Eliza and Taylor.

"What?" asked Eliza.

"I mean modeling professionally." Casey rolled her eyes. "You're not really into it, are you?"

"Why not?" asked Taylor. "I hear the money is pretty good."

"It's not about the money," said Eliza in a superior tone. Easy for her to say since her family was one of the wealthiest in the country. "I simply think it would be fun."

"What do your parents think?" asked DJ.

Eliza shrugged. "They think that it's nice that I'm learning to be a *lady*." She sort of laughed. "But I doubt they'd be too excited to see me taking modeling as seriously as your grandmother does. Still, I think it would be kind of exciting."

"I'd take it seriously," said Kriti. Then she frowned. "If I wasn't so short."

"You could still do print," said Eliza. She used her forefingers and thumbs to frame Kriti's face. "You would be great for cosmetic ads. They go for those exotic-looking girls."

Placated, Kriti smiled.

"Well, the only part of the fashion industry that interests me is design," said Rhiannon as she stood and pushed her chair in. "And I consider myself fortunate to have Mrs. Carter's influence to help me get where I'm going."

"And don't underestimate that influence," said Eliza. "My mother told me last night that Mrs. Carter still has some pretty impressive connections in both New York and Paris."

Taylor chuckled. "Yeah. Ms. Katherine Carter may be getting long in the tooth, but the old girl's not dead yet."

"We better get moving," said Eliza.

DJ groaned as she stood and reached for her cane. Her leg really was aching today. This fashion show might be a great big deal to some girls, but to DJ it was simply a great big pain. Everyone began heading for their rooms. But, as usual of late, DJ moved more slowly, clomping along like an old woman with her cane and big boot. When she finally reached the foot of the stairs, Eliza seemed to be waiting for her.

Eliza smiled stiffly at DJ as she placed a hand on her shoulder. "You know . . . despite what Casey or the others might say, I really was happy for you last night."

DJ blinked at her. "Seriously?"

"I really did think it was *sweet*."

Sweet? That word put DJ's teeth on edge. "You actually seemed kind of shocked at the time."

"Well, naturally, it was pretty surprising." Eliza flipped a silky blonde strand of hair over her shoulder and laughed. "I mean, only days ago, you weren't even a finalist. If memory serves, I think you actually put down the whole thing. I'm sure you didn't even want it . . . not like others might have."

"Like you, you mean?"

She shrugged. "I invested myself in the campaign. I thought it would be fun. My parents came to . . . well, you know."

"So, you think it's unfair that I won?"

"Oh no, DJ, I'm not saying anything like that." Another sugary smile. "Like I said, I think it's very sweet that you won." She nodded down to DJ's walking cast and cane. "I mean, you *obviously* got the sympathy vote."

DJ pressed her lips together and nodded. "Obviously."

"So, no hard feelings then?" Eliza smiled again. Such a perfect smile. Perfect teeth. Perfect hair and skin. Even perfect words. And yet DJ could never be too sure what lurked beneath the surface.

"No hard feelings from me," said DJ lightly. She grabbed the stair railing with one hand and maneuvered her cane with the other. Then she paused and looked at Eliza. "And your parents are really okay with it too?"

"Other than being a little shocked, they are perfectly fine. Like I already told everyone, they only came up here to show their support for me."

DJ began maneuvering up the stairs. "Well, that's a relief."

"Don't worry, DJ. They're still glad they came up. And, naturally, my mother cannot wait to see me in the fashion show today. Speaking of which, we better get moving."

"Right." DJ grimaced as she took another step.

"Do you need any help?" asked Eliza from behind her.

DJ continued clumping up the stairs. "No, I'm fine." She took in a sharp breath to block the pain shooting through her leg. "Just slow."

"Well, I'm sure you'll be the hit of the fashion show today. Not everyone gets to see a 'crippled' girl going down the runway. *Very sweet.*" With that Eliza passed DJ and gracefully jogged up the stairs.

DJ clenched her teeth tighter now. She was determined not to respond to that obvious slam. Really, what was the point? What difference did it make? Still, it was weird how some girls, like Eliza, could knock the wind out of you with just a few sweet-sounding, harmless words and a fake smile. And yet it hurt more than being punched or slapped. Freaky.

"Ready to get beautiful?" asked Taylor as DJ limped into their bedroom.

"Yeah, right." DJ made her way to the bed and dropped her cane as she eased herself down with a long sigh. "Do you really think anyone would miss me if I skipped it?"

"Your grandmother for starters."

"Maybe not . . ." DJ actually considered this. "I mean, she's really got her eye on you and Eliza. You guys are the ones with a future in fashion."

"You'd have a future too, DJ. If you wanted it." Taylor kind of laughed. "And if you weren't so handicapped."

"Those are big ifs. But, seriously, my grandmother will be so busy with everything else, she might not even notice my absence."

"Maybe not at first, but eventually she would realize you weren't there, DJ. And, think about it, then she would make you miserable for a few days. Is it really worth it?"

DJ shrugged. "I don't know."

"Come on. Just play along and get it over with."

"Fine. But first I'll take a pain pill and a nap."

"But I thought those pills wiped you out?"

DJ grinned at her. "Will it be my fault if I sleep too late?"

Taylor rolled her eyes as she headed for the bathroom. "It's your funeral."

2

viva vermont!

"come on, sleepyhead," said Taylor as she tugged on DJ's arm. "It's getting late, and we need to get you to look all pretty for the big show."

"I can't believe you were taking a nap," said Rhiannon.

DJ blinked sleepily. "What time is it?"

"It's time for you to get moving. That's why I called in the forces."

"I need to sleep," moaned DJ. That pill was still affecting her.

"You need to cooperate," insisted Casey.

And so, as DJ groggily sat on a chair in the center of the bedroom, Rhiannon, Taylor, and Casey all worked her over. Rhiannon did her hair. Although, what she was doing was a mystery to DJ. Not that she cared since Rhiannon was good with style. Taylor did DJ's makeup, which could be a mistake since Taylor was a little heavy-handed with the eye shadow at times, but, hey, it was a fashion show. And Casey actually did her nails. Who knew Casey (aka Grunge Girl) could do nails?

"Thanks, you guys," DJ said after they were done. Although she didn't want to look in the mirror. Why bother? She held out her hands. "Am I presentable now?"

"You'll pass," said Taylor. "Just don't let your grandmother get too close. Your complexion is really in need of some exfoliating."

Casey rolled her eyes, and Rhiannon handed DJ her cane.

"We're off to see the wizard," sang Taylor as they trekked down the stairs with DJ slowly bringing up the end of the line, "the wonderful wizard of odds."

Grandmother and the other girls had already left, and since they were running late, DJ opted to let Taylor drive.

"That's probably just as well," said Rhiannon as she and Casey got into the backseat. "Since you're obviously impaired."

"Are you on pain meds?" asked Casey.

DJ closed her eyes and leaned her head back, wishing that they would all be quiet so she could sleep. "Yeah ... I was in pain, okay?"

"I'm just jealous," muttered Casey. "I could use a little something for this fashion show myself."

"Casey!" snapped Taylor.

"Kidding," said Casey. "Well, sort of."

"How's your rehab counseling going?" asked Rhiannon.

"I'm doing the program, okay?" said Casey in a grumpy tone.

"And DJ is doing the drugs," teased Taylor.

"Are you going to be okay on the runway, DJ?" asked Rhiannon. "You're not going to pass out or anything, are you?"

"I'll be fine," said DJ, without opening her eyes. Sure, she was a little groggy, but at least her leg didn't hurt. "The sooner we get this over with, the happier I'll be."

"While you were snoozing, your grandmother gave us a copy of the lineup," said Rhiannon. "Eliza leads off the big show, and you follow."

DJ brightened some. "And then I'll be done. That's nice. Maybe I can sneak back to the car to sleep."

"That's so unfair," complained Casey. "At least you should have to stay and watch. I mean, the rest of us have to do the runway at least twice."

"I'm doing three," said Taylor, a trace of pride creeping into her voice.

"You really *do* like this, don't you?" Casey accused her.

"Sure, I like it. You know me. I *love* being admired." Taylor laughed that big husky laugh of hers. And DJ knew that she was simply stating a fact. Taylor did love being the center of attention — she went out of her way for the limelight. Well, vive la différence!

Casey groaned. "You make me sick."

"Whatever."

Soon they were there. The "models" were all cloistered in this stuffy room that had apparently been set up for brides, since Keller Tavern was a favorite wedding location. A couple of women from the Chic Boutique were supervising the clothes. And as far as DJ could tell, everyone was getting along and getting dressed. Of course, a simple thing like "getting dressed" wasn't a great challenge to most people. But for DJ — with a walking-boot cast and cane to maneuver about, combined with no place to sit — it was starting to feel like an Olympic event. She'd managed to get her hoodie jacket off, but was having a problem with her sweatpants. She was looking around for an inconspicuous exit when Rhiannon joined her.

"Looks like you need a hand," she said as she steadied DJ from toppling into the clothes rack.

"I was thinking more like I needed an escape route," admitted DJ.

"Oh, look," said Rhiannon as she removed some items that were bundled together on the rack. She pointed to the tag that said *Desiree Lane*. "Here's your outfit, DJ. Nice."

"Thanks a lot," said DJ. "The challenge of locating the clothes wasn't hard, it was figuring out how to get dressed without breaking my other leg." Just then a girl trying to pull up a pair of boots bumped DJ from behind, causing her to grab onto Rhiannon to keep from falling. "See what I mean."

"Let me help," offered Rhiannon as she balanced DJ and helped her out of her sweats. Then she unzipped the sweater dress. It was the color of warm sand and very soft. She slipped it over DJ's head, being careful not to muss her hair.

"What about you?" mumbled DJ from beneath the fabric. "Don't you need to get dressed too?"

"My first walk is number ten ... I figure I have loads of time. Wow, this cashmere is really nice," said Rhiannon as she zipped it. "And really sophisticated." She stepped back to admire it. "It's amazing how the simplest lines are the most elegant ... and the hardest to pull off too. It looks great on you, by the way."

"Thanks." DJ stood a little straighter.

"But not with your footwear."

So then Rhiannon helped DJ into a sleek dark brown Prada boot.

"I wouldn't mind a pair of these myself," said DJ as she longingly watched Rhiannon place the unnecessary boot back in the tissue paper. "I mean, when the cast comes off."

Rhiannon's eyebrows shot up as she noticed the price on the box. "Those boots cost $990."

"No wonder they've got security guards all around," pointed out DJ.

Next Rhiannon helped her with some large tortoise shell-beaded earrings, a long necklace, and a mix of bangle bracelets that actually looked pretty good together. "I'm liking this outfit," said Rhiannon as she fussed with DJ's hair again. "Very classic."

DJ shrugged. "Is that it?

"Hey," said Taylor as she joined them. "Looking good, DJ. But you need to freshen those lips." Before DJ could say a word, Taylor whipped out some gloss and put a layer on.

"You're looking good too." DJ laughed. "Black leather suits you. All you need now is a whip."

"I wouldn't mind wearing this outfit home." Taylor struck a pose. "Except that it would wipe out my clothing budget for an entire month. I just tallied it up, and the whole thing comes to about five grand."

"No way!" Rhiannon looked appalled.

"You might have the right idea, Rhiannon," said DJ. "I think designers make more money than models."

"But they don't get as many of the perks," said Taylor.

Rhiannon adjusted the wide leather belt on DJ's hips, setting it at an angle that DJ never would've considered. Then she stepped back and smiled with satisfaction. "You look fantastic, DJ."

"And the color of that dress is really good with your hair," offered Taylor. "Really brings out the gold highlights, which, if I may suggest, need to be touched up soon."

"Thanks." DJ nodded grimly. "But does this outfit go with my cane?"

Rhiannon laughed. "Don't worry, darling, no one will be looking at your cane today."

"No," said DJ, "they'll be looking at my boots."

Now Eliza joined them. "That's right," she said, snickering as she glanced down at the mismatched boots. The one sleek brown knee-high Prada, and the other, DJ's clumsy-looking black walking cast.

"Why are you picking on DJ?" demanded Rhiannon.

"Moi?" Eliza batted her thick eyelashes at them. Naturally, Eliza looked fabulous in a pair of fitted black pants and short boots with very high heels. This was topped by a black-and-white checked jacket with oversized buttons. Very sixties and very chic in a Jackie O kind of way. Not that DJ planned to tell Eliza as much after that last comment. Besides, Eliza was obviously aware that she looked good.

"She's picking on DJ because she's still jealous about losing to her last night," said Taylor with a smirk. "Eliza doesn't like to lose, do you, Eliza?"

Eliza's eyes flashed in what almost seemed hot blue anger, but then she took in a breath and smiled, and she even patted DJ on the back. "Don't worry about the fashion show, dear, you're certain to get the sympathy applause out there today."

"Thanks a lot," said DJ.

"By the way, you should be pleased to know that the proceeds from this fundraiser go to the Ronald McDonald House, DJ. I'm sure you'd fit right in with those poor handicapped kids." Eliza laughed and flitted away.

Okay, this made DJ mad. It was bad enough for Eliza to give her a hard time, but to make a comment like that was so out of line. DJ remembered the young girl at the Ronald McDonald House — and how she'd helped DJ get over herself. Maybe Eliza should spend some time with Lacy Michaels too.

Taylor made cat claws at Eliza's back, hissing for special effect.

"She's still really angry about not getting homecoming queen." Rhiannon shook her head. "Unbelievable."

"Unbelievably selfish," snapped Taylor. "I mean, she's not the only one who lost."

"But you were a good loser," said Rhiannon.

Taylor just shrugged. "Guess I didn't want it as badly as Miss Snooty Pants."

The music was beginning to play now, their cue that it was time to get ready. The feel of the music was very upbeat and energetic, probably in hopes that women spectators would feel like opening up their pocketbooks. The girls had practiced to this music already, but DJ had never been able to move and walk like the others. It was one thing to fumble about in the privacy of your own home, with only your "friends" to tease you. But doing it in public like this ... well, it would be humiliating. What a comedown from last night. Surely Eliza should get a small bit of satisfaction from that, shouldn't she?

DJ took in a deep breath as she hobbled over to get in line behind Eliza. It was bad enough to clump down the runway, but it figured that she'd follow Miss Supermodel Eliza Wilton. And, in the rush to get ready, DJ hadn't even remembered to put on deodorant. Great, now she was going to pit out a thousand dollar dress. She wondered if she had time to shove some tissues in her armpits, but figured it was unlikely since Eliza was already getting ready to go. Oh, well, best to just grin and bear it. Get it over with. ASAP.

Naturally, Grandmother was the emcee for the fashion show. After a short formal welcome and some introductions to some of the local supporters as well as the designers, she cleared her throat, and the runway music began to play again. The lights, which were operated by volunteers from the high school drama department, began to fan around, making the room seem even more high energy. Grandmother's intention had been to make this feel like a real New York event.

"And our first lovely model today is Eliza Wilton. Eliza is one of our Carter House girls, originally from Louisville. Her parents, Mr. and Mrs. Thomas Wilton, are joining us today." As Grandmother spoke, describing Eliza's outfit and the designer responsible, Eliza perfectly executed the pattern that the girls had been taught to walk—all the way to the end of the runway, turn, walk halfway back, turn again, back to the end, one last turn, and then back to the staging area.

The rest of the plan was that when the model did her final turn, the next model would emerge from staging. She would begin her walk so that the two would cross somewhere near the middle. "So the runway is never empty," Grandmother had instructed them. "That keeps the energy and excitement escalated. Like choreography."

So as Eliza made her last turn, accompanied by a hearty applause, DJ began her walk down the runway. But because she was slowed down by the cane and walking cast, she was only a quarter of the way before she and Eliza met. Eliza's eyes locked onto DJ's, and her pasted-on smile never even twitched as they passed. But as DJ took her next step, her cane somehow missed the floor. Realizing she was about to plunge forward on her bad leg, and trying to balance herself as well as to avoid pain, DJ did something like a tuck and roll. It was a movement the girls used to avoid a bad fall when making a dive for the ball in a volleyball match. Naturally, this carried her straight off the narrow runway and right into the laps of a couple of very startled-looking older women.

"Oh, my!" cried one as she looked down at DJ.

"I'm—I'm sorry!"

"Are you all right, dear?" asked the other woman.

Feeling like a complete fool, DJ struggled to get off as several other people attempted to help her. By then the music had quieted down, and DJ was certain that all eyes were on her. She was about to stand and take a bow, when she heard Taylor say, *"You witch!"*

DJ looked up in time to see Taylor holding onto Eliza by the sleeve of her checked jacket. "You tripped DJ on purpose. I saw you kick her cane!" And then, to DJ's shocked horror, Taylor slapped Eliza. The audience gasped. But that wasn't the end of it. Eliza, usually so composed and careful, now had eyes filled with rage, and she lunged back at Taylor!

Suddenly the two of them were actually fighting. Okay, it was that pathetic kind of girl fighting, where neither of them really knew what to do. Lots of slapping and grabbing and attempts to kick at each other. But it was definitely a fight. DJ could not believe her eyes.

"Ladies!" cried Grandmother from the podium. "Ladies! Ladies!"

"Are you okay?" asked a gentleman as he handed DJ her cane.

DJ nodded silently, but her eyes were still locked on Taylor and Eliza. Fortunately, they were being separated by several of the other models and some of the fashion show helpers. Grandmother was fanning herself with her notes and looked as if she might faint. How on earth was she going to get out of this little mess?

3

Viva Vermont!

BUT GRANDMOTHER, being Grandmother, managed to maintain her usual sense of style and confidence. She even attempted to make light of the fiasco, saying things like "girls will be girls." Then she asked the stunned audience to forgive the girls for their foolishness.

"I suppose they simply wanted to liven things up a bit," she said finally. "I had encouraged them to keep the energy up." She laughed, but it was an uncomfortable laugh. "And with that in mind, where is the music? I believe it's time to start this up." So the music began once again, and the next model emerged.

In the holding room, DJ realized that she never had completed her whole run, not that she cared. And certainly no one could blame her now. In fact, she felt fortunate that she hadn't been seriously injured.

"What happened out there?" asked Rhiannon with wide eyes. She was just finishing getting her outfit on. "I heard the commotion, but I was still in my underwear so I missed everything."

DJ gave her the lowdown.

"No way!" exclaimed Rhiannon as she slipped into her shoes.

Then Taylor joined them. "Can you believe what that witch did to DJ?"

"She really did that?" asked Rhiannon with disbelief. "She actually tripped her?"

"I saw her do it with my own eyes." Taylor glared over to where Eliza and her mother were now having what looked like a pretty heated conversation in a far corner of the room. "While DJ's cane was in the air, Eliza gracefully swung her foot directly at it, which is why the cane missed the floor and why DJ did her little acrobatic act." Taylor grinned at DJ. "That was quite a flip you did off the runway, Deej."

"You really did a flip off the runway?"

"I guess ... or more like a somersault ..." DJ was still watching Eliza and her mom and, although she couldn't hear anything, she could tell by their expressions that Mrs. Wilton was not the least bit pleased with her daughter. In fact, DJ suspected that the mother had observed Eliza's little stunt as well.

"Don't look now," DJ whispered, "but I think Eliza's mom is on her case for tripping me out there."

Naturally Taylor turned and stared, but fortunately not for too long. "Wonder of wonders ..." she said with some satisfaction. "I think you're right."

"Taylor Mitchell on deck," called one of the helpers from the front now.

"Come with me," demanded Taylor. Then she grabbed DJ by the arm and actually tugged her along.

"Why?"

"Because you still have to do the runway."

"But I—"

Taylor gave DJ no chance to argue. Before DJ knew what hit her, Taylor had tossed her cane aside, linked arms with her, and they were walking the runway *together*. There was no way DJ could get away without hurting her leg. Fortunately, Taylor paced herself so that DJ could keep up. Taylor held her head up with a smile that simply oozed confidence. And DJ, despite all her insecurities, tried to imitate her.

Grandmother looked surprised, but recovered quickly. "Well, isn't this sweet," she said. "Our lovely Taylor Mitchell is helping my own granddaughter, Desiree Lane. Such a thoughtful girl! Some of you may know that DJ recently broke her leg while rescuing a little boy . . . perhaps you read about it in the paper?"

The audience broke into applause now, and Grandmother looked extremely pleased with herself as she began to describe DJ's outfit in detail.

"It seems only fitting," said Grandmother as DJ and Taylor reached the center of the runway and paused, "that Crescent Cove's royalty should participate in today's fashion show. Some of you may have missed it, but Desiree Lane was crowned homecoming queen last night." More applause. And to DJ's relief, Taylor slowly maneuvered the turn, which actually turned out to be somewhat graceful.

Finally, after they finished their paces, Taylor escorted DJ back to the holding area. But DJ felt bad that there hadn't been time for Grandmother to describe Taylor's outfit.

"There ya go!" Taylor handed DJ her cane, then grinned and waved as she headed back out and did her own walk. DJ stood on the sidelines to watch. This walk was much faster, bigger strides, one foot in front of the other, and with such amazing confidence, she could've easily passed as a professional model. Even more pleased, Grandmother now gushed about Taylor. "And here's a little something you may not know," she added. "Taylor's mother is the famous jazz musician Eva Perez." The crowd seemed appropriately impressed. Then Grandmother continued to describe the outfit with enthusiasm as Taylor strutted back and forth. Naturally, this was followed by even more applause — in fact it seemed to be a thunderous applause — like maybe Taylor would be crowned queen of the fashion show. Not that she didn't deserve it. She probably did.

"Way to go," said DJ, giving Taylor a high five as she returned to the holding area. "You were awesome out there."

"Thanks. I better go change."

It seemed everyone in the room was moving at fast speed now. Girls were in various stages of dress, all hurrying to be ready for their next runway walk. And, despite all her complaints, DJ felt a little left out as she moved to the sidelines. Eliza's mother had disappeared, and a sulky Eliza was changing into her next outfit. She obviously had no intention of abandoning the fashion show. Or maybe her mother wouldn't allow it. Still, DJ wondered how Grandmother would react to her next run. Then again, knowing Grandmother, she wouldn't bat an eyelash. After all, Eliza was a beauty. Wasn't that all that mattered, really?

DJ glanced over to where Taylor was making final adjustments on a gorgeous red silky dress. She looked amazing. She notice DJ watching and tossed her a wicked grin, like she knew she looked amazing. DJ gave her two thumbs-up, and Taylor winked.

Okay, DJ had to wonder. Was it possible that Taylor had planned that whole thing simply to get some more limelight? Oh, not the part where Eliza tripped DJ, or how the two girls got into the subsequent fight ... but what about the sweet little escorting of the poor disabled girl down the runway? Did Taylor see her opportunity and snag it? Or was she genuinely trying to be helpful? Who could tell with someone like Taylor? And yet, DJ had been touched by the seeming act of kindness. She wanted to believe that Taylor really cared about her. Who knew that Taylor had it in her?

"Despite some young ladies' efforts to spoil things today, the fashion show was a total success," announced Grandmother at dinner that night. "We raised more money than ever before."

Everyone at the table clapped, including Eliza's parents, who had surprised Grandmother by joining them for dinner. DJ had overheard the intense conversation between Grandmother and the cook and housekeeper at the announcement late in the afternoon.

"We will be dining formally," she had informed them. "And I expect a delicious six- to seven-course meal." Well, the end result was calling out for catering service. Still, Clara and Inez were expected to put everything together and serve this meal "with perfection." DJ couldn't help but feel sorry for them.

This dining development came after the wealthy Wiltons spent about an hour "in conference" with Grandmother this afternoon. DJ knew that they were considering pulling Eliza from Carter House, and DJ had actually hoped that it would happen. Perhaps it would help to bring peace to their chaotic household. Because, despite Eliza's "sweet" smiles and compliments, she seemed to have a real streak of meanness beneath.

But after their conference, the Wiltons seemed somewhat appeased. How Grandmother had managed to reassure them that she was not running a sloppy establishment was a mystery. But apparently she had.

"Desiree," Grandmother had said quietly as she caught DJ heading upstairs that afternoon. "Please inform the girls that we are dining formally tonight. I expect them to dress accordingly, and I expect everyone to be on their best behavior." She frowned at DJ. "Is that perfectly clear?"

DJ shrugged. "Clear enough. I'll let them know."

Grandmother smiled then, patting her hair as if a single styled hair might possibly be out of place. "Thank you, dear. I am in need of a little rest."

So DJ had told the other girls what was up, and, although they had complained, everyone had complied. As they sat around the formally set table, DJ thought they'd all make a good ad for a food and fashion magazine, not that she knew of such a thing. Anyway, Grandmother should be appeased. General Harding had joined them as well, sitting at the opposite end of the table from Grandmother and looking very pleased with himself.

The turkey bisque soup had barely been served (and to DJ's relief, this was not tasting like their typical low-fat, low-cholesterol, low-calorie fare), when Eliza's mother used her butter knife to ding on her crystal glass. The table grew unusually quiet. "Excuse me," she said politely. "But Eliza has something to say to everyone."

Eliza sat up straighter and looked around the table with what seemed a contrite but not completely genuine smile. DJ got the distinct feeling what they were about to hear had been carefully rehearsed.

"I want to apologize to everyone," she began in her soft, lilting Kentucky drawl. "And particularly to Desiree." She smiled at DJ now. "I simply do not know what came over me today, except that I was probably having a severe case of pea-green envy." She sort of laughed, probably in what might be described as a "southern genteel" sort of way, but it grated on DJ's ears. "I am truly sorry for creating such a spectacle at the fashion show, and I hope that y'all can find it in your hearts to forgive me." Eliza looked at Taylor now, but DJ couldn't see her expression, only Taylor's, and it didn't look very convinced. "And I apologize to you too, Taylor. I should not have reacted as I did. Please, forgive me."

"Well, of course we forgive you, Eliza," said Grandmother happily. "As I said, girls will be girls. And although I'm training you girls to be ladies, I must remember that Rome was not built in a day. We have made progress, but we still have a long way to go yet." Then she turned to the Wiltons. "However, I was quite encouraged to hear from some of my New York friends. They were very impressed with the Carter House girls, and felt that some girls might have a future in the fashion industry."

Mr. Wilton frowned now. "It's fine for Eliza to learn to act like a lady, if that's actually the case, but we would never approve of her taking up modeling as a profession."

"Although she might dabble with it a bit," added her mother. "Just for fun." She smiled at Eliza now. "It does seem like fun, doesn't it?"

Eliza sort of shrugged. "Oh, I don't know . . . I doubt that anyone would take me seriously out there."

"Oh, don't be too sure of that," said Grandmother. "Based on some of the remarks I heard today, there is some very serious interest."

"Well, I'm far more interested in seeing Eliza maintaining good grades," said her father. "That's more important than fashion."

Grandmother looked slightly stunned, but said nothing.

"You must be pleased that Eliza got the starring role in our musical," said Kriti positively. More than ever, it seemed Kriti was Eliza's biggest fan.

"Really?" Mr. Wilton peered curiously at his daughter. "I hadn't heard about this."

"Oh, I thought I mentioned it to Mom."

"Which musical is it?" asked Mrs. Wilton with interest.

"South Pacific," said Kriti.

"Ooh, I loved that movie," gushed Mrs. Wilton. "Eliza, why didn't you tell me about it?"

"I thought I had." Eliza smiled and shrugged in what seemed faux humility.

"Eliza is playing the nurse," said Rhiannon.

"Nurse Nellie," offered Kriti. "And she's really good."

"Wonderful," said Mrs. Wilton. "I can just see you in that role, Eliza."

"Yes," said Kriti. "She's perfect for it."

"And I'm playing Liat," said Taylor, perhaps a little too smugly. "Remember the island girl who Lieutenant Cable falls for."

"Oh, yes," said Mrs. Wilton. "The talking hands song."

"That's right."

"And Taylor has a beautiful singing voice too," said Rhiannon, which DJ thought was unnecessarily gracious since Taylor had sort of blackmailed her way into a role that had originally belonged to Rhiannon. But to be fair, that was really Casey's fault. Whatever.

"When will the performances begin?" asked Mr. Wilton.

"The week following Thanksgiving," said Rhiannon. "Thursday through Saturday."

"Oh ..." Mrs. Wilton looked disappointed. "We'll be back in France by then." She glanced at her husband. "But maybe we could hop back."

He nodded and smiled. "We wouldn't want to miss it, would we?"

DJ wondered what it would be like to have a full set of "original" parents who were that interested in their daughter's life. Oh sure, they weren't interested enough *not* to put her in boarding school, but their willingness to hop across the Atlantic Ocean just to see her in the school play was impressive.

DJ felt an unexpected pang of longing now. Of course, she knew that if her mom was still alive, things would be different. Very, very different. But she also knew that it was out of her control, and all she could do was move on and make the best of it.

"Not to change the subject," said General Harding. "But I wanted to invite you girls to use my lodge next month."

"That's right," said Grandmother. "General Harding has generously offered us the use of his lodge for Veteran's Day weekend."

"And if we're lucky, there will be skiing by then," he told them. "I hear the forecast is for a lot of early snow this year. What do you girls think?"

"Ooh," said Eliza. "I love to ski."

"And I love to snowboard," said DJ.

"What about your leg?" asked Rhiannon.

DJ frowned. "Well, this cast is supposed to come off in a few weeks. Hopefully I'll get the green light."

Suddenly, the girls all seemed to be talking at once, making plans for what to take, what they needed to shop for, and which was better—skiing or snowboarding. It seemed to be split down the middle. Although Kriti, who hadn't done either, was naturally siding with Eliza. Anyway, DJ thought that perhaps the fashion show fight had been completely forgotten in all this excitement, which might be for the best. Especially since it seemed certain that Eliza wasn't going anywhere.

"And where is your lodge, General Harding?" asked Mr. Wilton after the table quieted down a bit.

"Vermont, of course."

"Viva Vermont!" said Taylor, holding up her crystal goblet of sparkling apple cider as if to make a toast.

"Viva Vermont!" echoed the other girls.

4

viva vermont!

WHETHER IT WAS THE SEEMINGLY endless rain or her clumsy cane and walking cast, the next couple of weeks seemed to move like molasses in winter for DJ. She was really trying not to let her "handicap" get to her, and she was trying not to be envious of the other girls as they went about their normal activities. She was actually praying quite a bit, as well as reading her Bible and going to church and youth group. But still it was hard not to feel a little bummed.

It didn't help matters that it seemed like everyone else in Carter House had 1) a life, 2) a boyfriend (or mostly), and 3) extracurricular activities to occupy their time—whether it was practicing for the musical, doing sports, or whatever. It always seemed that everyone, except DJ, had someplace to go or someone to see or something to do, including her grandmother, who had been spending a lot of time with the general lately.

DJ's one and only extracurricular activity (besides youth group) was to go to the pool three times a week to swim laps. Sure, she swam by herself while the swim team did their warm-ups and laughed and joked amongst themselves. But it was better than going straight home from school every day, and it helped to pass the time. Plus, the physical therapy was good for her leg. Or so the therapist assured her the last time she went for a visit, even though she hadn't allowed DJ to lose her walking cast yet. That was a bummer.

But lately DJ had been feeling like a soggy sponge (both inside and out). It seemed she was either hobbling through the rain, leaving the pool with wet hair, or trying to dry the moisture out of that stupid walking-cast boot. And then it felt like she was crying on the inside too—soggy, soggy. Okay, maybe crying was an overstatement. But she was definitely feeling depressed.

The only highlight of her life was seeing Caleb at the pool, and he hadn't even been there this past week. She'd asked Caleb's replacement about it and had been told that he'd taken a week off to go to his brother's wedding somewhere on the West Coast. She'd tried to act like "that's cool," but she really did miss him. Not that Caleb ever treated her as anything much more than a kid sister—a kid sister that he genuinely liked—but it had been nice having him around. And she missed looking at him, sitting there on the lifeguard chair, smiling that amazing smile, keeping an eye on everyone in the pool.

Sometimes, as a distraction to other things, she'd find herself daydreaming about Caleb, thinking about when she would graduate from high school (with honors!) and join him at Yale. Okay, she knew she'd have to get extremely serious about her studies if that actually were to happen. But having this forced hiatus from sports, and everything else she loved, proved to be a good opportunity to hit the books. Consequently, her grades did seem to be improving some. Ironic, since she had never considered herself to be academic. Having been the "sporty" girl for so many years, it was hard perceiving herself in a different light. But life had changed.

"You've sure turned into a bookworm," said Taylor one night as she was getting ready for bed.

"Crazy, huh?" DJ set aside her history book and yawned. "I used to hate doing homework."

"Pretty much." Taylor frowned as she adjusted a strap of her black silk nightie. The neckline was cut low enough to expose her ample cleavage—not that DJ cared to look. In fact, she still thought it was weird that Taylor wore these silky, slinky, sexy numbers every single night. Like who was she trying to impress anyway? DJ just didn't get it. The stuff Taylor wore didn't even look comfortable—let alone warm. But it's like Taylor never let her guard down when it came to clothing and style. Almost as if she and Eliza were in some kind of competition for "best dressed" Carter House girl. Actually, either of them could easily win that award at school as well. Perhaps in the whole town.

Despite DJ's attempts to improve her own fashion habits, she knew she would never take it to the level of Taylor or Eliza. In fact, when it came to sleepwear, Eliza was pretty much the same as Taylor. Although DJ had to give the girl credit since Eliza didn't go in for "sexy" stuff. Still, she wore "only the finest." And many of her expensive lace and embroidered nightgowns were from France. But she also shopped at Victoria's Secret when she was in the mood to go "slumming." Naturally, Kriti had started to follow suit too, although her taste leaned more toward classic silk pajamas. Still, they couldn't be cheap. DJ felt pretty sure that Taylor, Eliza, and Kriti kept Victoria's Secret in business.

Thank goodness DJ still had Casey and Rhiannon to make her feel normal when it came to fashion. As far as their sleepwear was concerned, they all stuck with their faithful tank tops, T-shirts, boxer-style bottoms, sweats, or an occasional nightshirt. Nothing involving silk, lace, or a fancy designer name.

"I never do homework," bragged Taylor.

"Yeah, I've noticed you never bring home books or anything."

"Why bother with all that stuff every day? I'm sure it can't be good for your back lugging all those books around." Taylor was brushing her hair and then twisting it into a smooth bun that was supposed to "prevent split ends" while she slept. She'd recommended that DJ do the same, although DJ wasn't sure how anyone could sleep with a big lump of hair to contend with. "Seriously, DJ, I don't know why you drag all that stuff home every day."

"Uh . . . have you heard of homework?"

"I do mine at school." Taylor opened a bottle of expensive-looking Estée Lauder cream and carefully massaged it onto her forearms and neck.

"How is that even possible?"

"Oh, there are lots of ways . . . mostly I just work fast. I complete a lot of things while I'm in class. And I actually use my study period to work." She laughed. "Well, mostly anyway."

"And you manage to keep your grades up?"

"*Yeah . . .*"

DJ frowned. "Okay, I don't get this . . . do you cheat or something?"

Taylor tossed DJ a scathing glance as she rubbed lotion onto her feet. "For your information, school has always been easy for me."

"Apparently." DJ returned her attention to her book. Still, she wasn't so sure. Someone with Taylor's kind of morals, or lack of, might not be above cheating. Not that DJ planned to make any accusations. Lately, she'd managed to stay on Taylor's good side. In fact, she'd lasted longer in that position than anyone else in this house. If she had to continue being roommates with Taylor, it was well worth practicing a little congeniality.

"Hey, Seth," purred Taylor into the phone. "What's up?"

Seth Keller was Taylor's latest boyfriend, if you could call the guys she dated "boyfriends," which might be a stretch. Taylor seemed to change boyfriends as often as most people changed their sheets. It seemed more appropriate to call them "casual encounters." Or maybe even road-kill, since she'd already left a trail of broken hearts behind — or so she seemed to think.

Taylor enjoyed going over her romantic history, when she could get DJ to listen. She would sit and number off her poor victims, one by one, on her fingers. Personally, DJ suspected that some of those guys might've been relieved to have made it out of Taylor's clutches in one piece. And, oddly enough, their old girlfriends usually took them back. DJ wondered if the girls didn't even feel sorry for the guys — like they'd been helplessly overcome by the evil seductress's spell and finally returned to their senses. Although, to be fair, it seemed that Taylor was always the one who ended the relationships — or conquests, depending on how you looked at it.

But DJ wondered if that might possibly change one of these days — maybe sometime in the foreseeable future too. Because last Saturday night, after Taylor had been out with Seth and probably drinking and doing who knew what else, she had actually admitted to DJ that her greatest fear was being dumped by a guy before she had a chance to dump him first.

"I have a need for control," she'd confessed while puffing on a cigarette by the open window. "I want the upper hand, you know?"

Well, DJ wasn't sure that she did know. In fact, for the most part DJ felt like she'd never had any control over any aspect of her own life. Well, other than herself and her own choices. She even attempted to say as much to Taylor, but it was obvious that Taylor wasn't listening ... and equally obvious that she only wanted to be listened to.

Taylor had also told DJ that she "really, really liked Seth," but that it scared her to feel that way about any one guy. "It makes me feel too vulnerable," she'd admitted. And, okay, DJ tried to sound sympathetic, but at the same time she wondered if Taylor had any idea of how shallow and selfish she was when it came to guys. More than that, DJ wondered what would happen if Taylor really was on the other end of the "dump" for a change. Would she fall apart? Would she expect DJ to pick up the pieces? DJ wasn't ready to think about that. In fact, DJ didn't want to think about anything that had to do with guys or romance or dating or anything like that. It was just too depressing.

"Let's have a Halloween party," suggested Rhiannon at breakfast.

"You can't plan a party *four* days in advance," pointed out Eliza.

"Why not?" countered Taylor.

"I think it sounds like fun," said DJ, eager to take Rhiannon's side against Eliza. "What did you have in mind, Rhiannon?"

"You know, just a fun old-fashioned Halloween party. We could dress up and dunk for apples and carve pumpkins and—"

"Go trick-or-treating?" teased Taylor.

"Not exactly." Rhiannon frowned. "But what's wrong with having some good old-fashioned fun? What's wrong with fixing some party food and decorating and putting together some costumes?"

"Nothing," said DJ. "It's a great idea."

"But Halloween is only four days away," repeated Eliza.

"Don't be such a wet blanket," said Taylor.

"Well, how do you send out invitations?" asked Eliza.

"Verbal invitations," said Rhiannon. "It's not unheard of."

"It sounds pretty childish to me," said Kriti. Again, it seemed she was taking Eliza's side.

"Well, you don't have to come if you don't want to," said Casey. "Maybe I'm childish, but I happen to think it'll be a hoot."

"Who's in favor of a Halloween party?" DJ asked suddenly. "Raise your hands."

DJ, Taylor, Rhiannon, and Casey all shot their hands up. Then, with reluctance Eliza and Kriti followed.

"It's settled," said Rhiannon. "Okay, today is Thursday, and Halloween is on Sunday. We'll have to start inviting people today. How about if each of us is allowed to invite four people?"

"That's only twenty-four guests, for a total of thirty, including us," said Taylor. "And that's if everyone comes, which is unlikely."

"Math whiz," teased DJ.

"Anyway, if about half of them came, which does seem likely, it would only be about fifteen people. And that doesn't seem like much of a party to me. I think we need at least forty to feel like it's a party."

"Uh, maybe we should check with my grandmother," suggested DJ.

"Yeah," said Taylor. "You do that, okay?"

"And I'll be in charge of decorations," continued Rhiannon. "I've already got some things I can use from art."

"And I'll help her," offered Casey eagerly.

"Back to how many guests?" persisted Taylor. "There's no point to start planning if you don't know how many you're planning for."

"Taylor's right," agreed Eliza.

Taylor looked surprised. "Why, thank you."

"Let me go find my grandmother first," said DJ. "She was going to a hair appointment this morning. I might be able to catch her."

DJ could hear the girls continuing to plan as she took off to search for her grandmother. It actually sounded like the enthusiasm was growing. And DJ did think it could be fun. She just hoped Grandmother would see it that way.

"Oh, there you are," said DJ. Grandmother was just slipping her handbag over her arm and about to go out the door. "Got a minute?"

"Just barely." She tapped DJ on the shoulder. "Stand up straight, Desiree."

DJ stood a bit straighter. "The girls want to have a Halloween party," she said quickly. "Is that okay with you?"

"Halloween?" Grandmother's brow creased. "When is that anyway?"

"Sunday."

"Oh ... well, I don't see why not. Perhaps a Halloween party would be fun for the girls."

"Okay, I'll tell them."

"Now I must be off, I'm running late."

"Thanks!"

By the time DJ got back to the dining room to announce the good news, it had all been settled. The party would start at seven. Everyone could invite eight friends for a total of forty-eight guests, plus the hostesses. Rhiannon and Casey were doing the decorations. Taylor was lining up some kind of music and planned to set up the seldom-used third floor as a dancing area. "We'll call it Club Ghoul," she suggested. And it seemed that the rest of them, meaning Eliza, Kriti, and DJ, were in charge of food.

"How are we going to pay for everything?" asked DJ.

"The decorations should be cheap," said Rhiannon. "I've got some ideas that really don't cost much."

"But what about the food?" persisted DJ.

"We'll all chip in," said Taylor.

"How much?" asked Rhiannon with a worried look.

"Since you're doing decorations, you shouldn't have to chip in for food too," said DJ quickly. She knew that Rhiannon was always strapped for money. "But how about the rest of us? How much does it cost to feed fifty people? And we're just talking party food, right? Not like a full meal deal."

"Just party food," said Casey. "And drinks, of course."

"But no alcohol," pointed out Rhiannon.

"Party pooper," said Taylor.

"Rhiannon's right," said DJ firmly. "No alcohol."

"Whatever."

"Could we do it for five dollars a person?" asked Kriti.

"That'd be about $250," said Taylor, "which is fifty bucks split five ways."

"I don't think you can do anything very nice for only $250," said Eliza.

"Well, you can always contribute more if you think we need *haute cuisine*," teased Taylor.

"Well, maybe I will."

"We need to get going," said Kriti, glancing at the clock. "Or we'll be late for school."

"So, it's settled. Everyone gets to invite eight people," Taylor reminded them as they left the table.

"And no booze," added Rhiannon. "Make sure the guests understand that too."

Taylor rolled her eyes. "Great, I get to invite my friends to a kiddy party."

Taylor would probably have no problem getting friends, particularly guys, since she was usually surrounded by several, to come to any kind of a party (booze or not). On the other hand, DJ wasn't overly confident that she even had eight friends to invite.

5

viva vermont!

"**wow, I can't believe** we're pulling this off," said DJ on Sunday afternoon. She stepped back to watch as Kriti and Eliza carried the large punch bowl out to the dining room table. She would've helped, but she'd only been out of her walking cast for a couple of days now and she still wasn't too sure of herself. Besides that, she wasn't too sure about the punch staying in the bowl as it sloshed back and forth. She expected to see the whole thing all over the wood floor any second. Fortunately, Inez had the good sense to remove the expensive oriental carpet earlier that day.

"I'm not going to be responsible for cleaning that," she had grumped to DJ and Rhiannon. "It's bad enough you girls are putting spiderwebs on every single thing in sight. Don't expect me to clean that up either."

"I think we should've put the bowl on the table before we filled it," said Kriti.

Eliza groaned as some of the strange gloppy green mixture of Sierra Mist and lime sherbet slopped out of the bowl and splattered onto the dining room floor.

"Don't worry, I'll get it," said DJ, using a black napkin to blot it up.

"Be careful, Kriti!" commanded Eliza.

"What's in that stuff?" asked Casey. She paused from where she was perched on a stepladder, stringing a spiderweb from the chandelier, to peer down at the weird green mixture. "It looks like snot."

"It's called Eye of Newt Punch," said Kriti as they finally settled it in the center of the table. "Whew."

DJ picked up a bowl full of frozen green gelatin balls and began plopping them into the punch.

"Are those Jell-O shots?" asked Taylor hopefully.

"No." DJ scowled at her. "They are just plain Jell-O balls disguising themselves as eyeballs. Get it?"

"Remember, this is a non-alcohol party," said Kriti sternly. "No booze."

After a disagreement — with Rhiannon and DJ against the rest of them — the girls had finally agreed to go with a scary theme for the party. "It's one thing to throw a Halloween party," Taylor had argued, "but if it's only pumpkins and bobbing for apples, you can count me out." Eliza, Kriti, and Casey had all agreed. Consequently, by Sunday afternoon, Carter House had been transformed into a haunted mansion. The food, according to Eliza, was supposed to be "creepy and weird, but tasty."

Eliza had taken charge of the menu. She'd found a Martha Stewart website, and their Halloween menu included things like Graveyard Cake, Witch's Fingers and Frankenstein Toes, Coffin Worms, Spider Nests, and other weird-looking items. By the time they were finished, DJ wasn't sure if anyone would actually want to eat this stuff since it looked like something that had been dug out of the backyard. But the general effect was spooky and fun.

Casey and Rhiannon had turned the front yard into a graveyard, complete with ghouls and ghosts. The backyard was outfitted with an apple-dunking tub and a pumpkin-carving table, although the weather had turned cold enough that it was possible no one would want to go outside. But at least it wasn't raining. The girls had set up the family room with old horror flicks and popcorn, and the third floor, "Club Ghoul," was all set for dancing. Taylor had hired a disc jockey who had agreed to come dressed as a vampire.

"Now we better get into costume," said Rhiannon. "Our guests will be here in less than an hour."

"That's only if they come on time," said Eliza as they were heading up the stairs. "Anybody who's anybody knows that you never come on time to a party."

"Even a kiddy Halloween party with no booze?" countered Taylor.

"Well ... I guess we'll see." Eliza actually smiled at Taylor.

Okay, Eliza and Taylor hadn't exactly been on friendly terms, but perhaps that was changing. DJ hoped so. It was hard enough living with five girls, but it was even harder when there was a big squabble going on.

"I hope we didn't do all this work for nothing," said Taylor as she and DJ went into their room.

"What do you mean?"

"I mean, what if no one shows?"

"Why would no one show?"

Taylor gave her a DUH look. "Because it's a *kiddy* party with no booze."

"I think it'll be fun."

"Yeah, well …" Taylor was getting out her costume now. She'd been keeping it secret, but she was going to be a witch, and DJ didn't think that would surprise anyone. But instead of an ugly witch with warts and bad hair, Taylor was going for the sexy, seductress type of witch. Well, no surprises there either.

DJ, on the other extreme, was dressing as a scarecrow. Naturally, Taylor thought her costume was juvenile. But DJ didn't care. She already had the overalls anyway. Together with a plaid flannel shirt, bandana, and a straw hat, it seemed pretty simple … and maybe a little lazy too.

Taylor shook her head when DJ emerged from the bathroom with a scarecrow face now painted on. "You look like you're about five years old."

DJ shrugged. "So?" Then she frowned at Taylor's outfit. "You look like a Halloween hooker."

Taylor gave her a seductive grin. "Hey, thanks! Just what I was going for. Tricks for treats."

"You're insane."

Taylor reached over and touched DJ's hair. The chlorine at the pool had been taking a toll on it lately. "Well, at least this straw hair goes with your costume, Deej. Nice touch."

DJ looked at herself in the mirror. Next to Taylor she probably did look like a five-year-old scarecrow with straw hair. But it wasn't as if she had anyone to impress tonight … and certainly no one she needed to look "sexy" for. Not that she'd do that anyway. But unlike the other girls (including Kriti!) DJ did not have a boyfriend coming tonight. Sure, she'd invited Caleb in an offhanded sort of way, and he'd been nice enough about it, but had — no surprises here — declined. Why would a college student want to come to a high school party? The truth was she wasn't too excited about the whole stupid party herself. She just didn't want anyone to know the real reason why.

DJ practiced making a scarecrow smile in the mirror. But it looked pretty pathetic. So she pulled out an eyeliner pencil and decided to go ahead and draw a smile right on her face. Okay, it looked slightly goofy and ridiculous, but she might need it before the night was over. As much as she tried not to show it or dwell on it, DJ was acutely aware that her ex-boyfriend (also her first boyfriend) Conner Alberts was coming to the party tonight. And she knew that he was bringing his new—make that old—girlfriend Haley Callahan with him.

Eliza had made that clear enough. "I invited Conner and Haley," she'd informed DJ. "I didn't see how I could not invite him. I mean, he is Harry's best friend. I just hope you're okay with that." DJ had acted like it was no big deal. But Eliza didn't stop there. "And just so you know, he is bringing Haley. I hope that's not a problem for you." Although DJ suspected that Eliza would be glad to create problems for her. Still, DJ acted like it was perfectly fine.

And it wasn't like DJ had to hang with the happy couple tonight. There should be plenty of guests to mingle with. Although she'd been trying to be nice to Haley lately, especially since Haley had reached out to her by giving rides to the pool during DJ's non-driving period. And DJ had told Conner, "No hard feelings." Still, it hurt to think of it—how it had felt to be dumped by him for Haley. But that had been DJ's little secret. As far as she knew, no one even suspected that she still had feelings for Conner. And that's just how she planned to keep it.

On the positive side, DJ's "broken heart" had been one of the main things driving her prayer life lately. She knew enough about being a Christian to realize that the best possible therapy was to give her sadness and disappointments to God. And she had no problem talking to God about this kind of thing—she knew he wasn't going to tell anyone. Plus, she always felt better afterward. And so, after Taylor went to check on the disc jockey, DJ spent some time praying. And, as usual, she prayed for the other girls in the house, finally coming to Rhiannon and her situation with Bradford.

That was the other recent development in the Carter House romance scene. Lately Bradford had been trying to win Rhiannon back. He'd sent her notes and flowers and had apologized many times over. But Rhiannon had been maintaining a "safe distance." She'd been patient with him, putting up with his attention in a tolerant and somewhat amused sort of way, but she always kept him at arm's length. Just the same, DJ had suspected all along that Rhiannon still liked Bradford. But maybe she simply wanted him to do penance or something that proved to her that he was really sorry for hurting her when he'd allowed Taylor to derail him.

In fact, Bradford had spent the past two days begging Rhiannon to invite him to the Halloween party. He'd already been invited by Taylor, which DJ felt was in bad taste. Taylor had assured them that she hadn't invited him to come for her sake since she was going with Seth Keller now. But Bradford rejected Taylor's invitation, telling everyone that he would only go to the party if Rhiannon invited him personally. And so she had finally caved at youth group the night before. Yes, Bradford had also been back in youth group. Poor guy, he really was trying to straighten out. So now it looked quite likely that Rhiannon and Bradford were seriously getting back together again. DJ just hoped that Bradford wouldn't hurt Rhiannon again.

Anyway, now it seemed that DJ, the poor scarecrow, would be the only Carter House girl without a boyfriend at the party tonight. She was trying to convince herself it was no big deal. And that she could always slip away to her room if she felt like a misfit, which seemed likely.

Rhiannon stuck her head into DJ's room. "Hey, we're supposed to head downstairs," she said. "Your grandmother wants to take a photo of all of us in costume before the guests arrive."

"Great outfit." DJ paused to admire Rhiannon's dramatic attire of flowing skirt and scarves and flashy jewelry. "Although I don't usually think of gypsies as having red hair."

"I'll bet there were a few."

"Anyway, you make a very pretty redheaded gypsy."

"Thanks. And Bradford is coming as a pirate."

"You guys will be a colorful couple."

Rhiannon smiled in a nervous way. "A couple ..."

"Are you excited about getting back with him?"

Rhiannon shrugged. "I'm just praying that it doesn't turn out like last time."

"It won't," DJ assured her. "Bradford learned a lesson."

"Let's hope so."

Now Rhiannon studied DJ's outfit with an unimpressed expression. "Hey, I could've helped you to put together a real costume, DJ."

"What's that supposed to mean?"

"Well ... it's not like you went all out."

"I happen to think it suits me." DJ swaggered toward the stairs now, breaking out into the old scarecrow song from The Wizard of Oz. "I would while away the hours, conversing with the flowers, if I only had a brain."

"Wait up," called Casey.

"No way!" yelled DJ when she saw Casey's costume. "Catwoman!"

Casey held up her hands like claws then hissed.

"Where did you get that outfit?"

"I ordered it online. It's a rental. Garrison is coming as Batman."

"You guys will be quite the dynamic duo."

"Yeah, it's probably a little over the top, but I've always dreamed of being Catwoman." Casey frowned at DJ now. "A scarecrow?"

"Yeah, yeah, Rhiannon's already raked me over the coals for my lack of creativity."

"Come on down, girls," called Grandmother. "The general is taking photos."

Grandmother was dressed up too. Like Taylor, she was a witch, but instead of a short black dress with a plunging neckline, Grandmother was a more dignified witch. Still, she had no warts or hooked nose.

"Line up, girls," ordered the general. He was actually wearing his general uniform, which was a little tight around the middle.

So they lined up with the others, and General Harding took several photos. "You girls look so pretty," he said after he finished. "Well, except for the farmer there." He chuckled.

"I'm a scarecrow," DJ corrected him.

"We can't even tell that you're a girl, Desiree," said Grandmother. "Surely you could've come up with something better than that?"

DJ looked at Eliza, who was "masquerading" as Miss America, complete with pink sequined gown and tiara. Then she looked at Kriti, who was wearing the belly dancer costume that Eliza had ordered online for her. Poor Kriti looked slightly uncomfortable and was showing way more skin than normal.

DJ just shrugged, pretending not to have been offended. "Well, at least I'll be comfortable."

"Good point," said Casey. "I'll be losing these spike-heeled boots before too long."

And before too long, despite Eliza's comments about how the fashionable always arrive late, the guests began to come. DJ decided to keep a low profile. Although Grandmother had asked Inez and Clara to manage the food and serving, DJ decided to hang with them and help.

"Why are not you out there with the partiers?" asked Inez.

"I'm not really into it."

"Why are you hiding your pretty figure beneath those hideous overalls?" asked Clara as she put more witch's fingers on a tray.

"I'm not hiding anything." Then, feeling like she didn't even fit in the kitchen, DJ decided to go out and mingle.

"Hey, DJ," said Haley, waving. She was dressed as a fairy princess, and Conner was a goofy-looking knight. Corny, but sort of sweet too.

DJ forced a smile and hesitantly approached the fairy tale couple. "You guys look cute," she said.

Conner seemed to grimace as he said a halfhearted "thanks," but Haley smiled brightly, then started to chatter on and on about what a great party it was ... how the decorations were so great and the food was ... blah-blah-blah. DJ was unable to focus on Haley's words. All she wanted was to get out of there.

"Excuse me," she said suddenly. "There's something I need to check on." Then she hurried through the dining room and out the back door. It looked as if someone had started to carve a jack-o'-lantern, but given up. No wonder, since it was very cold outside. So cold that DJ could see her breath.

She rubbed her hands together then picked up the knife. She was determined to finish carving a face into the abandoned pumpkin. Before long, she forgot all about the cold. Instead, she concentrated on cutting out a pair of surprised eyes and a pear-shaped nose and finally a nice toothy grin.

"There," she said to the finished jack-o'-lantern, "at least one of us is happy now." Then she took one of the votive candles from the supplies basket that Rhiannon had so nicely arranged. She set this inside her pumpkin and then lit it. Just as she was holding her hands over the flame to warm them, she heard the back door open and looked up to see a knight closing it with his back to her, almost as if he were sneaking out. She knew it was Conner, but she also knew it was too late to make a graceful getaway. So, without thinking, she picked up her freshly carved jack-o-lantern and held it up to cover her face, hoping that she might somehow pass herself off as a stuffed scarecrow in the dimly lit yard.

6

viva vermont!

"DJ?" **CONNER WAS WALKING TOWARD HER,** but she was not moving from her scarecrow stance. And she wasn't going to answer.

"I like your smiley pumpkin head, Scarecrow Girl."

She set down the jack-o'-lantern and made a sheepish smile.

"What are you doing out here all by yourself?" he said with way too much interest.

"I could ask you the same thing."

"It was getting stuffy in there." He took in a deep breath. "I needed some air."

"Well, it's cold out here," she said, making her way toward the back door. She did not want to be alone with Conner.

"Don't go yet ..." Conner came toward her now, actually removing his knight's cape as if trying to show some chivalry. And before she could stop him, he placed it around her shoulders.

"What are you doing?" she said, stepping away from him in shock.

"I just wanted to talk to you, okay?"

She shivered then pulled the cape more closely around her shoulders, absorbing the warmth as she waited for him to talk. But Conner didn't say anything.

"I thought you said you wanted to talk," she said in a slightly aggravated tone. Why was he doing this?

He looked down at the ground. "I don't really know what to say."

"Oh ..." DJ sighed and looked back at her jack-o'-lantern. With the twinkling candlelight, he seemed to be winking at her. Perhaps he knew something that she didn't. Or perhaps he was warning her to make a fast break.

"I guess I just want to say I'm sorry."

"You already said that, Conner. And like I said, it's okay. It's over and done and I don't even—"

"No, I don't mean I'm sorry about that—about breaking up with you. Although I am sorry."

"What then?" She turned and looked directly into his face. Whatever this game was, she wished he'd get on with it.

"I mean I'm sorry ... as in ... I miss you, DJ."

She forced what felt like an awkward smile. "Well, you can still talk to me. And we can still be friends, right?"

"Right ..." He slowly nodded, but he seemed unconvinced. And he was frowning.

"Look, Conner, Haley is a really nice girl. And I know you guys go way back. And I really do understand why you decided to—"

"No, you don't understand. Haley is nice enough. But she's not you, DJ. I miss you."

DJ blinked. "Really?"

"Yes. You and Haley ... well, you're so different. And I thought I wanted to get back with her, but now I'm not so sure. She's not like I remembered her. And she talks all the time, but she doesn't really say anything. You know?"

DJ shrugged. "Not really ..."

"I think I made a mistake."

"Oh ..."

"But I don't know what to do about it. And I really don't want to make a mess of things again ... and I don't want to hurt Haley."

Suddenly DJ felt angry. *He didn't want to hurt Haley?* What about the way he had hurt her? Why was he doing this to her now? And why was she even out here talking to him? Where was Princess Haley anyway?

"I'm cold," she said quickly. Then she removed his cape, handed it back to him, then turned and ran into the house, slamming the door behind her.

As she hurried through the crowded house, it was obvious that the Halloween party was still going strong. It seemed that there were even more people now than there had been before. Not that DJ was counting heads exactly, but she suspected that some of the "invited guests" had invited others as well. And Grandmother and the general were nowhere in sight. Also, judging by the way some of these kids were acting, someone had sneaked in some booze. DJ was tempted to test the punch to see if it had been spiked, then realized she didn't even care. There was nothing she could do about it anyway. Hopefully this party would end soon.

DJ slipped into the darkened family room where an old horror flick was playing. She thought this might be a good place to lurk in the shadows. But the seats were already taken by an audience of couples who seemed to be more into making out than watching the movie. She backed out of there and headed for the stairs. Mostly she just wanted to keep a low profile.

She decided to check out the dance scene on the third floor. The bass of the music was thumping away along with the sounds of dancing feet—more noise than this house had experienced for as long as DJ could recall. She walked into Club Ghoul and looked around. There seemed to be at least fifty people, and the dance floor was crowded and active.

Not that she wanted to dance, but she'd hoped that she might "disappear" into the crowd for a while. But it was hot and noisy, and, after being outside, the air in the house felt more stale and stuffy than ever. She considered going back downstairs and just hanging in the library, but worried she might run into Conner again. Or, even worse, Conner with Haley. And then what would she say? How would she act? She wondered if she'd even understood Conner correctly. Perhaps she had imagined the whole thing. But, even so, she didn't want to take any chances of running into Knight Conner and Princess Haley again. She just couldn't take it.

Besides that, her leg was starting to ache, and she missed her cane. Going up and down these stairs was not helping either. Finally, she decided simply to call it a night and go to her own room and just crash. She needed a quiet place where she could sit undisturbed and think about what Conner had actually said to her. She wanted to sort it all out. She wanted to replay their conversation and attempt to figure out what he was really trying to say, as well as how she felt about it.

But she had barely opened the door to her room when she heard noises coming from Taylor's side. DJ flicked on the light to see Taylor, the seductive witch, and Seth, the warlock, minus his pants, going at it on Taylor's bed. Disgusting! Totally disgusting!

DJ groaned and turned off the light. She started to leave, then stopped herself in the doorway. No way! This was her room! This stupid pair was not going to drive her out!

"Excuse me!" she said loudly, turning on the light again. "But this is my room, and I am not going anywhere!" Then she marched into the bathroom and turned on the light in there as well. She left the door wide open and continued to talk, loudly. "Some people need to respect other people's space. There are rules in this house, and whether you like it or—" Then she heard the door slam and went out to see that Taylor and Seth had evacuated.

"Good riddance," she said as she locked the door. But when she looked over at Taylor's rumpled bed, she noticed a clear vodka bottle on the bedside table. On closer inspection, she saw that it was nearly empty! Had Taylor and Seth consumed that much alcohol? If so, wouldn't they be feeling sick by now? She dumped what was left down the sink and just shook her head. Taylor was asking for trouble! Serious trouble. Not that there was much that DJ could do about it. Well, besides pray for her messed-up roommate. Not that it seemed to have done Taylor much good yet. Perhaps that was where faith came in … although DJ doubted she had that kind of faith.

Naturally, DJ did not feel the least bit sleepy now. For one thing, she was enraged at her foolish roommate. But besides that, she felt angry at Conner. What right did he have to say that to her? She knew she hadn't imagined it. It just made her mad to think of how he was jerking her heart around again. And why was he doing this? Why did he have to go and say that to her?

Despite herself, DJ felt a tiny bit sorry for Haley now. Did she have any idea how Conner felt? And if she did find out, would she blame DJ for this? Would she think that DJ had set out to win Conner back? Did DJ even want Conner back? Oh, what was wrong with people anyway?

DJ took her time turning off the alarm clock the following morning, but Taylor didn't even flinch. So DJ went over to make sure the girl was still breathing.

"Sounded like you were worshiping the porcelain throne last night," she said loudly. Taylor groaned and rolled over.

"Time to get up, roomie!" Now DJ pulled back Taylor's comforter, grabbing her by the arm in an attempt to drag the wasted girl from her bed.

"Leave me alone!" Taylor growled.

"Rise and shine," DJ sang at her. "It's a school day and you need—"

"I don't care!" Now Taylor spat some colorful words at her.

"Hey, watch the potty mouth," DJ warned as she grabbed both of Taylor's hands, pulling her into a sitting position. "It's time to get ready for school."

"I'm sick," whined Taylor. "I can't go to school today."

"Fine," DJ snapped as she went to retrieve the empty vodka bottle. She held it up for Taylor to see. "If that's the case, I'll go get my grandmother and show her exactly why it is you're so sick. And then maybe we can send you someplace to get some special kind of treatment for your unfortunate illness."

Apparently DJ's threat worked, because Taylor eventually joined them at the breakfast table. Although she wasn't touching her food, not even her coffee. And, judging by her greenish-looking skin tone, she was probably on the verge of hurling. But DJ didn't care. She had no sympathy for Taylor. Or for Eliza for that matter. It was obvious that both of them had been drinking last night, and that was after everyone had agreed to "no booze."

The dining room had been somewhat restored to its former self, but the rest of the house looked pretty bad. And both Inez and Clara did not seem the least bit pleased.

"That was quite a party last night," said Grandmother with a stern expression.

"We had party crashers," said Eliza in an apologetic tone. "We didn't know what to do about it, Mrs. Carter. Somehow the word got out that there was a party here, and people we never would've invited showed up."

"That is why it's best to send invitations," said Mrs. Carter, "and to have them presented at the door."

"That's exactly what I tried to tell the girls," explained Eliza. "But they felt that word of mouth was acceptable."

Grandmother shook her head. "Well, I hope you have all learned a lesson from this."

"And we can clean things up," offered Rhiannon. "After school."

The other girls nodded, everyone acted very contrite, and Grandmother seemed appeased. "Fortunately, there was no serious damage to the house," she continued. "But I do think I will call in a cleaning service."

Now all the girls looked relieved, but DJ was irked. It seemed unfair that Grandmother was letting them off this easily. Not that DJ relished the idea of cleaning up after a bunch of uninvited guests—guests that were probably more connected to Taylor and perhaps even Eliza than they were to the other girls. But just the same, there would be some satisfaction in seeing Taylor and Eliza down on their knees scrubbing toilets or mopping the floor. It seemed only right that they should take some responsibility for putting the house back together. But that was not to be the case.

The Carter House Halloween party was the talk of the school. DJ couldn't help but notice how Eliza and Taylor and

61

even Kriti seemed to be basking in this new form of limelight. Well, whatever. Mostly DJ was trying to avoid seeing Conner. Her plan was to remain aloof . . . to wait and see how he would handle this. Or if he even would. More than anything, she didn't want to be cast as the girl who had come between him and Haley. She didn't want to be blamed if—and it was a big if—they were to break up.

But the day passed without a word or even a glance from Conner. As she got into her car to drive to the pool, she started to wonder if perhaps she had imagined the whole thing. But when she got to the pool and saw Haley with red puffy eyes—and that was before she'd even gotten into the overly chlorinated water—DJ suspected that something was wrong. Still, as she tugged on her swimsuit, she was determined not to become a part of it. Really, it had nothing to do with her.

As she walked through the locker room, she could feel eyes on her. And she glanced over her shoulder in time to see Haley talking quietly amongst her swim team friends—and all of them were watching her with what seemed to be open hostility.

"Hey, Sunshine," said Caleb as DJ adjusted her swimming goggles over her cap.

"Hey, Caleb." She forced a smile.

"What's wrong?"

She shrugged. "You know . . . stupid high school stuff . . . the games people play . . ."

He nodded in a compassionate way. "Someday it'll all be just a memory, DJ."

"Here's to hoping." Then she jumped into the pool, waved at him, and started to swim. As if taking out her frustration on the water, she swam hard and fast. Soon her complete focus was on each stroke and each kick. DJ had decided that swimming was not only good for her leg, but kind of fun as well. Like any other athletic endeavor, it was a great way for her to forget about her troubles. Maybe that's why she liked sports so much. Finally, her hour was up, and she climbed out of the pool.

"You're turning into a really good swimmer," Caleb told her as she reached for her towel. "You should go out for swim team."

She laughed. "I don't think they'd be too interested in me."

"Don't kid yourself," he said. "I was watching you today. You're faster than some of the girls on the team." He chuckled. "Some of the boys too."

"Well, thanks for the compliment." She smiled up at him as she toweled off her face and hair. "But I still think I'll pass."

Fortunately, the team was still doing drills as she showered and dressed. She knew that she didn't want to see them talking about her again. But she was curious what Haley had told them about her. And she felt slightly indignant too. Even if Conner had broken up with Haley, which was DJ's guess, it wasn't like it was her fault. She certainly hadn't encouraged him. Maybe he hadn't broken up. Maybe DJ had imagined that they were talking about her. Maybe she was just getting paranoid.

Her phone rang as she walked out to her car. To her surprise it was Conner.

"I'm guessing you heard by now."

"Heard what?" she asked innocently.

"About the breakup."

"Breakup?" She unlocked her car and got inside, turned on the ignition, and waited for the heat to come on.

"Yeah, I broke up with Haley at lunch today."

"Oh ..." DJ felt a mixture of feelings. Part of her was glad, but another part of her was slightly worried.

"She wasn't too happy."

"I noticed."

"You saw her?"

So DJ described how Haley had looked in the locker room. She also described the hostile glances she'd gotten from Haley's friends. "Does Haley think I have something to do with you breaking up with her?"

"Sort of . . ."

"What do you mean sort of?" DJ felt anger in her voice now. "I didn't have anything to do with it, Conner. You know that."

"Well, I just told Haley the truth."

"The truth?"

"About how I feel about you, DJ."

DJ was too stunned to say anything now.

"I told her that I still liked you . . . that I had never stopped liking you . . ."

"You told her that?"

"Yes. And I told her that I'd been kind of blindsided by her. I mean, the way she was suddenly back here, and the way she kind of assumed we'd get back together . . . and it's like I wasn't thinking straight."

"But you're thinking straight now?"

"Yeah . . ."

"Oh . . ." DJ put the car into reverse. "Well, I'm driving, Conner. And I'm not supposed to be on the phone, you know . . ."

"Right. Can I call you later?"

She paused now. Maybe it was for effect. Or maybe it was because she was unsure. But she let him hang for a minute. "I guess so."

"Thanks. Later."

She closed her phone and started to drive toward home. Really, what was she setting herself up for now?

7

viva vermont!

THE MERRY MAIDS DID NOT LOOK any too merry as they packed up their van to leave Carter House. DJ couldn't help but feel sorry for them as she opened the front door. Really, who would want to clean up after a rowdy teen party, especially one where booze had been snuck in? As she went into the house, which smelled surprisingly fresh and clean, she knew she should be thankful that Grandmother had not forced the girls to clean up after all.

"Your grandmother wants to see you," Inez told DJ just as she was about to go into her room.

"Right now?" asked DJ.

Inez frowned. "Yes. Right now. She's in her room. And she's not pleased."

DJ dumped her bag, closed the door, and then went and stood in front of her grandmother's door. She wondered what was wrong.

"Go ahead. Knock," snapped Inez from behind her.

"I was going to." DJ rapped on the door and waited until her grandmother opened it.

"Oh, it's you," she said with a look of disappointment.

"Inez said that you—"

"Yes, yes . . ." She shook her head in a dismal way. "Come in. And close the door behind you."

Grandmother's suite, as usual, was perfection. Everything in the sitting room was varying shades of white and pale blue, and everything was in its place.

"Sit down."

DJ sat on a pale blue chair, and Grandmother sat on the white sofa across from her, still looking at DJ with an expression of deep disapproval.

"What is wrong?" demanded DJ.

Grandmother reached down behind the large ottoman that also served as a coffee table and produced an empty vodka bottle. "Inez found this in your room this morning."

"So?"

Grandmother's eyebrows shot up. "So?"

"It's not mine."

"Inez said it was on your bedside table, Desiree."

"Yes. It was on my bedside table because I had poured it down the sink last night." DJ wasn't sure how much she should say now. On one hand, she felt slightly and strangely protective of Taylor. On the other hand, what if Taylor had a serious drinking problem? What if she, like Casey and the pain pills, needed some kind of intervention?

"And why was it even in your possession, Desiree? Why, if what you're saying is true, did you pour it down the sink?"

"Because I found the bottle in my room and I didn't want it there."

"You found the bottle in your room?"

"Yes." DJ was shooting up a silent prayer now, begging God to show her what the right thing to do was. And suddenly it seemed clear. Simply tell the truth. "I'm surprised that you haven't figured it out yet, Grandmother, but—"

"Figured what out?" Grandmother leaned forward with interest, like she thought she was about to get some sort of confession from her wayward granddaughter.

"That some of the girls in this house might drink."

"What are you suggesting, Desiree?"

"Okay, I'll cut to the chase, Grandmother. Taylor drinks sometimes. She was drinking last night. So much so that she got sick. Couldn't you tell by looking at her at breakfast?"

Grandmother seemed to consider this.

"I don't know if she has a drinking problem or what, but I do know that she drinks sometimes. And I heard her throwing up at about four in the morning."

Grandmother frowned with disgust.

"And since you're somewhat responsible for the girls, well, it seems like you should be aware of what's going on in this house."

"Well … the party did seem to be a bit out of hand last night," she admitted. "Perhaps it's time for me to speak to all the girls—go over the house rules once again."

"That might be good."

Grandmother frowned at DJ and held up the bottle again. "Are you certain that you had nothing to do with this?"

"I told you the truth, Grandmother. I do not drink!"

She blinked. "I think I believe you."

"You should believe me."

Grandmother cleared her throat. "I suppose that's all then, Desiree. I will do as I see best to deal with the situation."

"Good." Then, feeling excused, DJ stood. But then she paused. "You know, Grandmother, the girls in Carter House may try to act all grown up, but they still need some guidance. I don't think you should just let everyone do as they please so much."

Grandmother seemed to consider this, but then she scowled. "Well, I expect the Carter House girls to be more mature than their peers. Theirs is a unique situation, and they have a responsibility to see that their behavior is appropriate. I am not here to babysit them. After all, ladies should be ladies."

DJ wanted to say, "Yeah, right . . ." and roll her eyes, but fortunately she controlled herself. Seriously, what was the point? Grandmother might be full of high ideals and fancy words, but the truth was the old woman was totally clueless when it came to raising teenagers.

"Still," mused Grandmother as DJ headed for the door, "perhaps we are due for some more fashion and etiquette training. I did promise Eliza's parents that we would focus on these things."

"Oh, yeah," said DJ under her breath. "That should fix everything." And how fair was that? Thanks to Taylor's stupidity, DJ was going to be tortured with more etiquette and fashion sessions. Maybe she should've just pretended like the vodka bottle was hers. She sighed loudly as she opened the door to her room.

"Hey, there you are," called Rhiannon. "Conner is downstairs."

"What? Why?"

"He's waiting for you."

"He's here?"

Rhiannon nodded with a curious expression. "So what exactly is going on between you guys anyway? I thought he and Haley were still—"

"He broke up with Haley today."

"Oh?"

"Yeah. And I'm pretty sure that Haley thinks it's my fault too."

"Maybe it is." Rhiannon gave DJ a sly smile. "Anyway, he's waiting."

DJ braced herself as she slowly went down the stairs. She had told him it was okay to call her ... not to show up in person.

"Hey," he said as she joined him in the living room.

"What's up?"

"We need to talk." He smiled. "And I didn't want to do it on the phone."

DJ glanced around the room. "I'm not sure that I want to do it here."

"Want to get a bite?"

Okay, did this guy know her or what? Naturally, she was starving as usual. And the prospect of a low-cal, low-fat dinner, combined with a possible lecture from Grandmother on how ladies should act like ladies, made DJ feel eager to get out of there ASAP.

"Let me grab my coat," she told him.

Soon they were driving in his old red pickup, and for a moment, DJ thought that maybe they had never broken up after all. Maybe they were still a couple. But then she remembered Haley. "Are you worried that someone might see us together?" she asked him suddenly. "And tell Haley?"

He shook his head. "Like I said, we broke up."

"Yeah, like a few hours ago. Is this going to be considered a rebound romance?" And even as she said this, she wished she hadn't. "Not that I'm saying there's any romance involved," she said quickly.

"It's not as if Haley and I were married, DJ. Yeah, we were going out, but I had figured it out a while back ... I mean, that it wasn't working. And I'd been trying to drop hints."

"Drop hints?" Okay, DJ was feeling mad again. "It's not like you dropped hints with me, Conner. As I recall you dumped me without any warning."

"I didn't dump you."

"Maybe not technically. But only because I beat you to the punch after you were seen kissing Haley. But it felt like I was dumped."

"Maybe it felt like I was dumped too." He gave her a slightly wounded look now.

"Right. And the next thing I knew you and Haley were an item."

"And I've told you that was a mistake. And I'm sorry. I'm really sorry, DJ."

"And now you want to get back with me?"

He smiled hopefully.

"Aren't you a little bit worried that you might be coming across as kind of flaky?"

His smile faded. "You think I'm flaky?"

"Yeah, maybe a little."

Now he actually laughed. "See, DJ, that's why I like you. You're not afraid to speak your mind. And you're not always all sweet and cheerful either."

"You mean you like me because I'm a grump?" She glared at him now.

"I like you because you're you, DJ. You're not afraid to be yourself." He sighed. "You're real."

"So are you saying that Haley isn't real?"

"No ... and I don't even think she's being phony. I just think she's a little too happy."

"Well, if it makes you feel any better, I don't think she's too happy right now. I saw her at the pool and I could tell she'd been crying. How does that make you feel?"

Conner didn't say anything now. DJ felt a little guilty as Conner parked in front of the Hammerhead Café.

"Okay, I'm not trying to make you feel bad," she said. "But I guess it's kind of a reality check. Haley seemed pretty devastated. She wasn't her usual cheerful, chatterbox self. How does that make you feel?"

"Sad."

"Sad enough to get back together with her?" DJ actually held her breath now, bracing herself for his answer.

But he just shook his head. "No, I don't want to get back with her. But I wish there had been a way to break up without hurting her."

They got out of the truck and went inside. But even as they ordered, DJ felt uncomfortable. "How would Haley feel if someone saw us together right now?" she asked.

Conner sighed. "Probably not much worse than she's already feeling." He looked at DJ with a hopeless expression. "I don't know what to do. Have I made this an even worse mess?"

"I don't know . . ."

"I just wanted to see you, DJ."

"I know . . . I guess I wanted to see you too. But I don't like feeling like the boyfriend-stealing girl—I don't like thinking that being with you right now is going to hurt Haley even more. You know?"

"What if we're only here together as friends, DJ?"

She considered this. "Yeah . . . friends . . ."

"In fact, that's what I wanted to talk to you about."

"About being friends?" She frowned now. This was starting to sound like some weird kind of rejection. Not that she had wanted them to be a couple per se. She didn't even know what she wanted.

"I've decided to give the whole dating thing a break. But I still really like you, DJ."

"Meaning?"

"Meaning I want to spend time with you, but I don't want it to turn into that old thing, you know?"

It took her a moment, but suddenly DJ got it. Conner was talking about what had ruined their relationship last summer—after the first time they'd started dating. It was that hot steamy scene in the car and how they'd both been uncomfortable afterward. So uncomfortable that they'd broken up, and she'd been hurt. She did not want to replay that again. "I don't want that either, Conner."

He looked relieved. "See, that was part of the problem with Haley."

"You mean she wanted to ... well, you know?" DJ felt her cheeks growing warm as the waitress brought their sodas.

"I think Haley thought that we'd stay together if we had sex."

"Did you?" Part of her wished she'd kept her mouth shut, but part of her had to know the answer.

"No, of course not."

"Of course not?"

"You know me, DJ. I don't want to go there."

She sighed with relief now. "I think you must be about the only seventeen-year-old boy in Crescent Cove, or maybe the planet, who doesn't."

"I'm not saying I don't *want* it—I'm just saying I want to wait. I really do want to follow God's plan for my life. Now more than ever."

DJ smiled. "Wow ... that's great to hear, Conner."

"And being with Haley ... it just wasn't cool."

"But being with me is?"

"I think you get me, DJ. Besides, I just like being with you."

"Kind of like a guy friend?" DJ felt slightly offended now. Was this his way of saying that she was "safe" because she was unattractive?

"No, DJ. Not like a guy friend. But like a smart girl who knows how to be in a relationship without losing her head. You know?"

She nodded. "Yeah, I think I do know." Thankfully, their fish and chips arrived then, and she changed the subject to her grandmother and how she had accused DJ of drinking vodka, and how DJ had actually caught Taylor and Seth in bed last night.

"No way."

She laughed. "Yep. Pretty disgusting too. I think they were both totally wasted. And Taylor got pretty sick. I even told my grandmother about it, but once she accepted that I wasn't the culprit, it almost seemed like she didn't care."

"Maybe she was just relieved that it wasn't you, DJ."

"I doubt that." DJ took a bite.

"She's an odd one, that grandmother of yours."

"You got that right."

It was weird, but cool, sitting there just eating and visiting with Conner again. Kind of like old times, but maybe even better. Sort of like some of the pressure was off. She just hoped that Haley would be okay.

8

viva vermont!

"YOU'RE JUST IN TIME for the big meeting," said Casey as DJ came into the house. "Your grandmother wants everyone in the living room at eight o'clock sharp, which is like now."

DJ rolled her eyes as she took off her jacket. "I know what this is about."

"What?" whispered Casey.

"Oh, you know ... ladies being ladies ... that sort of thing."

"Yeah, right." Casey peered at DJ now. "Rhiannon told me you were with Conner. Is that really true?"

So they hovered in the foyer, and DJ gave her the quick lowdown.

"Seriously, you guys are just going to be friends?"

"Sure, why not?"

"*Why not?*" Casey gave her wicked grin. "Because it's impossible."

"We'll see." DJ wanted to point out that she and Conner were both Christians, whereas Casey was still floundering when it came to her faith. Also, she was dating a guy who wasn't a Christian. Who knew what those two had been up to last night? Although DJ suspected their constricting superhero costumes might've made disrobing a challenge.

"By the way," DJ lowered her voice as they got nearer the living room. "Part of Grandmother's spiel tonight will involve alcohol. You weren't drinking last night, were you?"

Casey held up both hands. "No way. I'm still in therapy, remember?"

"Yeah, I remember. My point was, do you remember?"

Casey looked offended now. "Yes. And my counselor happens to think I'm making real progress—thank you very much."

DJ patted her back. "Well, good, Casey. That's great."

"But there was alcohol here last night," Casey whispered as they stood by the closed door. "Someone spiked the Eye of Newt Punch, and I know that some of the guys sneaked some stuff in."

"Too bad."

Casey shrugged. "What did you expect?"

"I don't know … I guess I wish some people would just grow up."

"Some people think that drinking is the way to grow up."

"Or throw up."

Casey laughed so hard she snorted, and, naturally, that got DJ giggling too. But they both stopped when they went into the living room and felt Grandmother's icy gaze directed toward them.

"I see you decided to join us."

"Sorry." DJ gave her grandmother a little finger wave. "But I was out. I didn't know there was a meeting."

"Sit down, please." Grandmother cleared her throat. "As I was saying, I expect you girls to conduct yourselves as mature young ladies. It's a privilege as well as a responsibility to live in a house such as this. And I do not want to feel that I am being taken advantage of. As a result of some of my findings in regard to last night's party, I feel that everyone is in need of a crash course in deportment."

"What is deportment?" asked Casey.

"Manners," said Grandmother. "And before I take you girls up to the general's lodge, which is in question just now, I expect you to prove to me that you are capable of practicing good etiquette. I also expect you to display mature and sound thinking. And speaking of sound thinking, it has come to my attention that some of my Carter House girls have indulged in alcohol, which you all know is strictly against the Carter House rules. Rather than pointing out the offenders, I will give you this severe warning. *Underage drinking will not be tolerated in this house. Is that understood?*" She narrowed her eyes, peering at the group in her most stern and austere expression.

The girls seemed to agree to this. Then Grandmother continued to ramble on and on about how she'd seen some models with perfectly good potential throwing away their lives on drugs and alcohol. "That is why we will have no tolerance for it in Carter House. Your parents have entrusted you girls to my care, and I do not intend to disappoint them."

DJ was sitting next to Taylor on the couch. She noticed that Taylor's eyes were closed. Not a big deal since Taylor often did this when bored. But then DJ could tell by her deep breathing that Taylor was asleep. She gave her a sharp jab with her elbow.

"Ouch!" Taylor jerked her head up and turned to glare at DJ.

DJ just smiled and looked directly forward.

Finally, Grandmother seemed to have run out of hot air. But not before she pulled out the Carter House rules and slowly and painfully read them.

"All girls must attend school, maintain above average grades, and respect the school district rules.

All girls must respect house curfew, which, unless otherwise agreed upon, is nine o'clock on school nights and eleven o'clock on non-school nights.

All girls are welcome to use the public areas of the house (living room, library, dining room, kitchen, and observatory) until ten o'clock on school nights and midnight on non-school nights.

All girls will refrain from smoking, drinking, or any form of substance abuse or other illegal activity.

All girls will refrain from unsavory speech, swearing, and general crudeness.

All girls will maintain their appearances and practice good etiquette at all times.

All girls will treat each other with respect.

All girls will conduct themselves with modesty and respectability both in private and public.

All girls will be responsible for their personal belongings and keep their bedrooms relatively neat.

All girls are expected to participate in fashion, etiquette, and style training sessions.

Any girl who breaks these rules is subject to loss of privileges and possible expulsion from the Carter House."

She folded the paper in half and looked evenly at the bored group of girls. "Have I made myself clear?" The girls all said yes and nodded once again. And finally, it seemed they were done.

"Good grief," said Eliza as they were going upstairs. "It's almost ten o'clock, and I still have homework to do."

"That was the most boring two hours of my life," complained Casey. "She's even worse than the pastor of my parents' church."

"I had a nice little nap," said Taylor smugly. "Well, until DJ had to go and spoil it."

"Who knew the old gal could go for so long?" said Eliza.

"It's her form of punishment," DJ pointed out. "And if you don't like it, why not just obey the rules."

"Or don't get caught," said Taylor as they reached the landing.

"You're the one who got caught," said DJ.

"What?" Taylor frowned at her. "I did not."

DJ rolled her eyes. "Yeah, whatever."

But once they were in their room, Taylor didn't let that comment go. "What do you mean I got caught?"

So DJ told her about the vodka bottle.

"Well, that's your fault. I would've tossed it out if it had been on my side of the room. I can't believe you left it just sitting out like that." Taylor laughed. "It's probably a good thing you're not a drinker, DJ. You're not very sneaky."

"Thanks, I'll take that as a compliment."

"Whatever." Taylor narrowed her eyes now. "Hey, back up the truck a minute. You said that I was the one who got caught, DJ. But you're the one who got called into your grandmother's office. What do you really mean?"

DJ just shrugged and headed for the bathroom. But before she could open the door, Taylor was blocking it. "Did you rat me out?"

"What difference would it make if I did? My grandmother obviously isn't terribly concerned."

"She was concerned enough to give us a long lecture."

"A lecture that you slept through."

"I was tired …" Taylor sighed and held her hand to her forehead dramatically. "I had a rough night last night."

"Look," said DJ. "It's not like I want to see you getting into trouble, Taylor. But I am worried about you. Did you and Seth split that whole bottle of vodka between the two of you?"

"Of course not."

"It was almost empty when I found it."

"Almost? Meaning you finished it off yourself?" Taylor gave DJ a wicked grin. "You little sneak, you."

"No, I did not finish it off. I poured it down the sink."

"Too bad. That was the good stuff."

"But, seriously, Taylor. Did you and Seth drink all of that?"

"No, of course not. You don't think it was a full bottle, do you?"

"I don't know what to think."

"It wasn't full, DJ."

"Where did you get it?" DJ knew that was a dumb question. All the girls knew that Taylor had a phony ID. She could've gotten it anywhere.

"Seth brought it. And, if you must know, he sneaked it from his parents' liquor cabinet. And it was only about half full."

Okay, that sounded pretty convincing. But DJ knew that Taylor could lie her way out of anything. And, this was one of those times when DJ did not believe her.

"May I please use the bathroom now?" she asked Taylor in an impatient voice.

"I suppose … but no more ratting out your roommate, DJ."

"Why would I even need to?" she tossed back as she pushed passed Taylor and went into the bathroom.

"Why indeed."

DJ shut the door and sighed. How long would she have to put up with Taylor's tricks? On one hand, she'd almost started to like the girl and on some levels even trusted her. But on the other hand, Taylor was maddening. And she was unpredictable. A real loose cannon. DJ knew that unless Grandmother caught Taylor with a bottle of booze in her hands, or unless Taylor got into some serious trouble at school or with the law, which seemed unlikely, Grandmother would probably continue to play oblivious. And DJ knew why. Grandmother's highest hopes for grooming one of the girls into a professional model rested in Taylor. For that reason, DJ suspected that Grandmother would turn a blind eye to most anything.

To aggravate Taylor, DJ took a long time in the bathroom. She knew that Taylor had her "beauty routines" and would probably be sitting out there fuming at DJ. But DJ did not care. Let her fume.

Finally, when DJ couldn't think of one more reason to remain in the bathroom and was actually feeling a bit silly, she went out to find that Taylor was sound asleep—on top of her bed, with her clothes on. Well, she really must've been worn out from last night. Feeling a little guilty, DJ dug out a soft wool blanket and draped it over her roommate, then turned out the light. Poor Taylor ... she really was her own worst enemy. But why?

The next day, DJ and Conner sat together at lunch. Of course, they were with their other friends too. But even so, DJ could feel the stares they were getting. And, naturally, Haley was nowhere to be seen. Who could blame her?

DJ didn't see Haley anywhere until Wednesday when she spotted her at the pool. But she was already in the water and never even looked up as DJ walked past. Unfortunately, that wasn't the case with Haley's friends. They had no problem staring at DJ and, DJ suspected, gossiping behind her back. Well, let them, she thought. It wasn't as if she'd done anything wrong. Still, she felt bad for Haley.

"Have you talked to Haley at all?" DJ asked Conner when he picked her up for youth group on Saturday.

"No, why?"

"I just wondered. Do you think she'll be at youth group?"

"I don't know why not. She seemed to like going before. But that might've just been because we were together then."

But, as it turned out, Haley wasn't there. That made DJ feel even worse. And so she decided that she would make an attempt to speak to Haley on Monday. She remembered how Haley had taken the time to smooth things out with DJ when the tables had been turned. Maybe it was DJ's turn now.

But when Monday came, DJ didn't see Haley around. And when she went to the pool after school, she discovered that Haley had switched over to doing the early morning practice.

"Not that she likes getting up that early," said Amy, one of Haley's less hostile friends, which wasn't saying much. "I mean who does?"

"Then why is she doing it?" Of course, DJ instantly regretted this when Amy tossed her a withering look.

"Why do you *think* she's doing it?" snipped Amy as she continued to towel dry her hair.

"To avoid me?"

"Duh."

"But I don't see why she'd—"

"Because you are poison," spewed a chunky girl named Bethany as she stepped right into DJ's space. She was one of Haley's toughest protectors, and DJ suspected that this girl might want to punch her right now. DJ took a cautious step back, holding her towel in front of herself in a defensive stance.

"I didn't do anything," said DJ calmly.

"Yeah, right," said Amy.

"Nothing besides stealing Haley's boyfriend," added Bethany. "And that's after Haley thought you were her friend. I can't believe I let Haley talk me into voting for you for homecoming queen. You are such a phony."

"A phony?"

"Yeah, a real hypocrite."

"A hypocrite?"

"You act like you're this nicey-nice Christian girl, and then you go and do that to Haley—just stab her behind her back. But then all you Carter House girls are like that. Haley should've known better than to trust you."

DJ blinked. "I didn't do anything to Haley. Conner and I are just friends. Ask anyone."

"We don't need to ask anyone," said Bethany. "Everyone knows what you are, DJ. *Poison.*"

DJ knew there was no point in continuing this. She also knew she didn't want it to escalate into something really crazy. So she simply walked away. But as she went into the locker room, she could hear them talking about her. Calling her "poison" and "backstabber" and ridiculous things like that. Even so, it hurt. DJ couldn't wait to get out of there. In fact, she decided as she hurried to dress, maybe this would be her last swimming day. Her leg was actually starting to feel pretty good now. Maybe she could find another form of strengthening exercise to continue her physical therapy.

She was just heading out of the building when she heard someone calling her name. Thankfully, it was a guy's voice or she might've taken off running. Seriously, she wasn't too sure about that Bethany girl.

"Hey, DJ," called the guy who coached swim team. He was waving and jogging toward her like he needed to tell her something important. Hopefully, he wasn't going to get on her case over Haley too.

"What?" she turned and looked at him with a slightly defensive expression. Seriously, what was wrong with these people?

"I know that you're DJ Lane. And I'm Coach Reynolds. Anyway, I've been watching you swim lately." He broke into a friendly smile. "You're looking really good out there."

"Oh ... thanks."

"And I think you could be a real asset to our team."

"Oh, I don't know ..."

"I realize you were swimming just to strengthen your broken leg, but I'm thinking anyone who can swim like that, just barely out of a cast ... Well, you're a natural, DJ. I'd love to have you join the team."

Okay, DJ was seriously flattered now. "Really?"

"Yep. And because you've been swimming most of the season, I think I can make the exception and let you join. The season is half over, but there are still some important meets left. And I'll bet you could pick up some medals."

"Oh, I don't know about—"

"Trust me, DJ. I was watching. You've got the right stuff."

"Wow ... well, thanks. But I haven't swum competitively since I was thirteen."

"But at least you've done it. That's great to hear. So you'll join us then?"

"I'll give it some thought."

He patted her on the shoulder now. "I'll keep my fingers crossed."

She smiled. "Anyway, I appreciate you thinking I could do it."

"Sure you can do it. But you'll have to start coming to practice every day. That alone might take you to the next level. Plus it'll keep you in shape for soccer. I know you're a good soccer player too."

She thanked him and felt surprisingly encouraged as she walked to her car. The fact was she had been enjoying swimming lately. And she really didn't want to quit. Plus, Coach Reynolds was right about the need to train and get in shape for spring soccer. She knew that basketball was out of the question. And sports were still important to her. It was also important to stand up for herself. She couldn't just slink away if a girl like Bethany trashed her in the locker room. That wasn't like DJ at all. So she decided she would do it. She would accept the challenge and go for it. Maybe somewhere along the way, she could straighten things out with Haley.

9

viva vermont!

"I THINK THAT'S GREAT," said Conner. DJ had just told him about her decision to join the swim team.

Today would be her first day to actually practice with them, and suddenly she was feeling a little uneasy. "I wonder what Haley will think."

Conner frowned. "I think you spend way too much time worrying about what Haley will think, DJ. You're a good athlete and from what I recall, our swim team is in need. Haley said they haven't won a meet yet. I'm sure she and the others will be glad to have you on the team."

DJ wasn't so sure. "I hope you're right."

Conner patted her on the back. "Of course I'm right. You'll be fine."

But as DJ drove toward the pool, she was still feeling uneasy. It was bad enough that she was being blamed for "stealing" Haley's boyfriend, but to trespass onto Haley's turf by joining the swim team might be asking for real trouble. She just hoped that no one would try to drown her.

As she walked across the pool parking lot, she was having some serious misgivings. Maybe this was a big fat mistake.

"Hey, DJ," called a voice from behind her. She turned to see Coach Reynolds jogging her way again, only this time he had a big grin. "Why don't you make my day and tell me you're here to join the team."

"Actually, I think I am."

"Fantastic!" He gave her a high five. "See ya inside." Then he jogged on ahead of her.

Okay . . . so there was no turning back now. She'd told him she was on board, and DJ wasn't the kind of girl to say one thing and do another. Still, she felt uneasy as she got into her suit.

"Hey, I heard the good news about you joining the team," said Caleb as DJ hovered nervously around the swim team area, watching as other team members did stretches and began getting into the water. "Coach Reynolds is stoked."

"I hope the rest of the team is okay with it."

"Oh, you mean because you're the newcomer?"

She shrugged as she adjusted the strap on her goggles. "Yeah . . . something like that."

"Hey, there she is," said Coach Reynolds as he joined them. "Our new star."

"Well, that's an overstatement," said DJ.

Coach Reynolds grinned then turned serious. "I guess we'll see about that. Now get into the pool and get warmed up. I want to do some timing today."

DJ chose the outside lane and tried not to look at anyone as she got into the water and began to swim. Just focus on your stroke, she told herself as she started to do the crawl, her strongest. First she swam slowly and evenly, then after a couple of laps she began to speed up. It felt good to slice through the water. She felt strong as she blocked out everything but the movement of her arms and legs. This was great.

The shrill sound of a whistle got her attention, and she realized that the coach was calling the team together. She quickly made her way to the pool's edge and climbed out.

"First of all, I want to introduce everyone to our newest team member, DJ Lane. I realize she's a latecomer, and I expect everyone here to help her to get with the program."

"Amy," he said, pointing his clipboard in her direction. "You work on starts and turns with DJ. She's a good enough swimmer and she's competed before, but it's been awhile, and my guess is she's a little rusty. Most of all, we need her to be ready for next weekend's meet."

Amy didn't look too pleased, but she nodded and said, "Okay."

"Time for drills," he said, then blew his whistle, and everyone began jumping into the pool. DJ followed suit. At least Amy got into the same lane with her. Maybe that was a good sign.

After about fifteen minutes of drills, Amy told DJ that her turns were all wrong.

"That might be because of my bad leg," said DJ as they clung to the edge of the pool.

"Or maybe you just don't know how to do them right," said Amy in a slightly haughty tone.

"Yeah, I'm sure that's possible. How about if you show me the right way?"

So Amy demonstrated and then watched as DJ practiced.

"That's a little better, but you're still slow."

DJ forced a smile. "Guess I'll just have to keep working on it."

Then they worked on dives, which fortunately DJ was still pretty good at. After about a dozen, she felt confident.

"But you still need to practice your turns," said Amy.

"I will." DJ forced another smile. "I appreciate you helping me."

Amy didn't respond, just dove into the water and continued with her own practice.

"Okay, DJ," said the coach. He had his stopwatch ready now. "Let's get some times down for you. How about you start with freestyle?"

DJ got on the starter block and waited for the sound of his whistle then dove. Okay, it wasn't as smooth as she'd have liked, but she didn't let that distract her as she swam hard. She knew that her times probably wouldn't meet the coach's expectations, but she'd give it her best shot.

He timed her in all the events, and, not to her surprise, she was slow in butterfly and breaststroke. Her strengths were crawl and backstroke.

"I want you to work on butterfly and breaststroke for the rest of practice," the coach told her.

She nodded, but felt disappointed. Those were her least favorite events. It seemed a waste of time to work on them. Still, after years of competitive sports, DJ knew better than to argue with a coach.

"Hey, Turtle Girl," said Bethany after DJ climbed out of the pool and removed her goggles and cap. "You're not moving too fast. You sure you can cut it on the team? Maybe you should go back to the handicapped lane before you totally humiliate yourself."

DJ wanted to point out that butterfly was her weakest stroke, but decided to ignore Bethany instead. Really, what was the point?

And, in the locker room, DJ kept to herself as well. She knew that the other girls, even Amy, were barely tolerating her presence. She also knew that as soon as they told Haley, which they surely would, it would probably get worse. She'd already overheard Bethany loudly complaining about how much they missed Haley at afternoon practice.

"I know," said Amy. "Let's all start practicing in the morning."

The other girls groaned, and DJ quickly stuffed her wet things into her duffle bag. She wanted to get out of there ASAP.

"Come on," urged Amy. "As a sign of solidarity to Haley."

Fortunately, DJ escaped before hearing the girls' response to Amy's suggestion. Well, whatever. Who cared if they all decided they wanted to get up at five a.m. to do an early practice? Besides, she seriously doubted that was going to happen. She suspected that even Haley would tire of it eventually.

"Your hair looks terrible," pointed out Taylor as DJ hung her suit in the shower to dry.

"Thanks."

"Seriously, DJ. You need to take care of it before it all breaks off. Have you ever heard of conditioner?"

"For your information, I do use conditioner."

"Well, that chlorine is ruining your hair." Taylor picked up a strand of DJ's hair and frowned. "Do you even wear a swim cap?"

"Yes. But it still gets wet. There's not much I can do about it. Maybe I'll just cut it."

"Cut your hair?" Taylor looked stunned. "Are you kidding?"

DJ shrugged. "I don't know. It would make it easier for swim team."

"Swim team?" Taylor frowned now. "Don't tell me . . ."

"Yeah. I joined the swim team. Aren't you proud of me?"

"You're nuts, DJ."

"Thanks."

"Okay, here's my best tip for you."

"A swimming tip?" DJ looked curiously at Taylor. "Do tell."

"No, not a swimming tip. Get real. A beauty tip."

DJ rolled her eyes.

"Condition your hair before you swim."

"What do you mean?"

"Coat your hair with a heavy conditioner, then put your cap on over it."

DJ nodded. That actually made some sense.

"The conditioner will help to protect your hair from the chlorine and then you can rinse it out, shampoo, and recondition. Understand?"

DJ laughed. "Or what? You'll refuse to be seen with me?"

"Yeah . . . maybe."

"Hey, DJ, where are the rest of the girls?" asked Marcus Wakefield. He was captain of the team and actually a fairly nice guy.

"They did morning practice today," Coach Reynolds answered for her.

"Why?" asked Marcus.

The coach peered curiously at DJ now. "I'm not sure why. I thought maybe they had some girls' event going on this afternoon. You know what's up, DJ?"

"Not really," said DJ. Okay, not totally true, but not a lie either.

"Well, looks like you'll be queen for the day." Coach Reynolds laughed then pointed to the pool. "Get busy, Queenie."

It was rather nice not having the other girls around to stare at her or make "Turtle Girl" comments. And the guys pretty much treated her like an equal even if most of them were faster.

92

Still, it was a good challenge trying to keep up with them, and by the end of practice Coach Reynolds seemed pleased.

"Looking good out there, DJ."

She thanked him then hurried to the locker room where she rinsed the conditioner (Taylor's recommendation) out of her hair, taking her time to shower and shampoo and condition again. Then she had the locker room to herself, and she decided she didn't care if the girls all continued to practice in the morning for the whole season. This wasn't half bad. She even decided to dry her hair for a change, taking advantage of having the whole mirror to herself. She took time to put on a little bit of makeup—just blush and lip gloss and mascara—but Taylor and the other girls might appreciate the effort since they'd all been on her case lately.

She took her time walking to her car. It had been one of those fine, crisp, clear fall days, and she knew they were limited.

"Hey, DJ!" called a guy's voice. She looked over to see Conner getting out of his old red pickup and waving. "I was hoping to catch you here."

"What's up?" she asked as she walked over to join him.

"Not much. But I was wishing for someone to grab a cheeseburger with me. You game?"

"You're talking my language."

He nodded. "I know the way to your heart is through your stomach."

She frowned now. "And you're trying to get to my heart?"

He looked uncomfortable. "No . . . I was just kidding."

They decided to drop her car off at Carter House, then she got in with him and he drove them over to a new diner called Heathcliff's. "Have you tried it yet?" he asked as they went inside.

"Nope. But it sure smells good."

They had just gotten seated and placed their order when DJ saw some girls coming in. "Oh no," she groaned and slumped down slightly in her seat.

"What?"

"Don't look now, but trouble's heading our way."

"What kind of trouble?"

"Haley and Bethany and Amy."

He just shrugged. "No big deal. It's a free country, and there are plenty of tables."

"Well, look who's here," said Bethany. "Cheating ex-boyfriend and backstabbing Turtle Girl."

"That's not very nice," said Conner.

"What makes you an expert on nice?" demanded Amy.

Haley just stood there staring at the two of them. "So it really is true then?"

"What?" Conner's brows lifted.

"You guys are already a couple?"

"No," said DJ. "We're just having—"

"I know what you're having," hissed Haley. "The whole school knows." She frowned at DJ. "And I actually thought you were a friend."

"I am a—"

"A backstabber," said Bethany.

"You guys deserve each other," said Amy.

DJ was about to remind them that Haley had been the original boyfriend stealer, but it looked like Haley was on the verge of tears, and the other two girls ushered her away. Then, instead of getting a table, they left.

"That's a relief," said Conner.

"A relief?" DJ peered at him. "We just got told off, and you think it's a relief?"

"Oh, I think girls get carried away sometimes and—"

"Girls get carried away?" She narrowed her eyes at him. "That's a little chauvinistic, don't you think?"

He nodded sheepishly. "What I meant is that some girls blow things way out of proportion. When Haley doesn't get her way, she can be a real drama queen, if you know what I mean."

DJ considered this. "I wouldn't have thought that."

"Well, you don't know her as well as I do. I mean, she can come across as real nice and sweet . . . as long as things are going her way. But you rock her boat, and watch out."

"Meaning I need to watch out?"

"Well, not you personally." He grinned. "Okay, enough about Haley. How about you? Tell me how practice went today."

So she told him about the girls' boycott, but how it was actually sort of nice.

He laughed. "No wonder they all looked so grumpy. They've been up since the wee hours of the morning. That's quite a sacrifice."

"Well, no one is making them do it."

"Probably won't last long—once they figure out that they're only hurting themselves."

DJ frowned. "I just hope they don't get together and decide to drown me in the diving pool. I was actually imagining them tying weights to my ankles and dumping me in there when no one was looking."

"Ugh, that's gruesome, DJ."

"You're telling me."

"Don't worry," he assured her. "It'll all blow over by the end of the week."

10

Viva Vermont!

BUT BY THE END OF THE WEEK, it had not blown over. Haley and friends were still doing morning swim team practice and taking jabs at DJ whenever they got the opportunity. Bethany had bumped into DJ by the lockers, knocking her so hard that DJ had a bruise on her upper arm. This whole thing was starting to scare her.

"Maybe I should just quit swim team," she had said to Casey and Taylor on Thursday night. It hurt to say this, especially considering that she'd just received her team suit that afternoon, but she wondered if it might not be for the best.

"Yeah, well, duh." Taylor took a long drag from her cigarette. The three of them were sitting out on the front porch, drinking diet sodas and smoking. Well, Casey and Taylor were smoking. And, in Casey's defense, DJ was pretty sure that Casey was just faux-smoking since she'd pretty much given up the nasty habit for volleyball season.

"You mean you'd let them bully you into quitting something you actually like doing?" demanded Casey. "That's just wrong."

"Yeah," agreed Taylor. "That is wrong. Even though I think swim team is lame, I think you should have the right to do it if you want."

"Maybe I don't want ..." DJ took a sip of her soda.

"And maybe you do," said Casey.

"Well, if I end up being dredged out of the bottom of the diving pool with lead weights tied around my ankles, you guys will know who to blame."

"That's a lovely picture, DJ." Taylor rolled her eyes.

"Yeah ... I know. Conner assured me that this thing with Haley would blow over by now, but it's not going away. If anything, I think Haley's just digging in deeper. And the swim meet on Saturday could really turn ugly."

"Maybe you need bodyguards," said Casey. "Want us to come and watch your meet?"

"Conner already offered," admitted DJ. "But I'm afraid that could make it even worse."

"Hmm ..." Taylor actually seemed to be considering this. "I suppose there would be some hot-looking guys there, right?"

DJ shrugged. "Yeah, I guess."

"In those little Speedo suits?"

DJ sort of laughed now. "Always on the prowl, aren't you, Taylor."

"I like to keep my eyes open."

"What about Seth?" asked Casey.

"What he doesn't know won't hurt him."

"So, what time is the meet?" asked Casey.

"It starts at eight in the morning," said DJ. "I'm not sure how long it'll go. But the coach said at least until noon."

"How about if we come and watch you do your thing," said Taylor, "and then we can do some shopping afterward."

"Shopping for what?" asked DJ.

"The general's ski trip," said Taylor. "You know it's the weekend after next."

"That's right," said DJ. "I nearly forgot. I still have to check with my physical therapist to see if it's okay to do a little snowboarding."

"And did Eliza tell you the good news?"

"What good news?"

"Harry's renting a cabin up there for the same weekend."

"Oh?"

"And he's inviting some of his buddies to join him, including Garrison and Seth." Casey winked at Taylor.

"Really? I hadn't heard about this." In fact, DJ wasn't too sure how she felt about this new little development. It was one thing doing a ski weekend with the Carter House girls. Even that had potential to get a little crazy. But throwing their boyfriends in as well . . . now, that could get downright scary.

She wondered if her grandmother had any idea what was going down, but at the same time realized that was highly unlikely. DJ also knew it was unlikely that she would tell the old woman. And equally unlikely that Grandmother would be too concerned even if she did know.

"I'm sure Conner will get an invite too," Taylor assured DJ.

"So next weekend should be extra fun," said Casey.

"I just hope I can survive this weekend first." DJ let out a dismal sigh.

On Friday, DJ considered foregoing the football game.

"But why?" Conner had demanded as they stood outside in the school parking lot. "That's like letting Haley and her thugs win."

She rubbed the bruise on her arm as she considered this. "Yeah, I suppose you're right."

"And the more you stand up to them and live your life, the sooner they should get bored with their little game."

"I just don't want to take any more hits from Bethany."

"Trust me, you won't have to." He gave her his tough-guy look now. "I've never struck a girl and I don't intend to, but I wouldn't hesitate to block one of her punches."

DJ laughed. "Well, thanks. Maybe you should come to the pool with me now."

"I thought you said the girls were still doing the morning shift."

"They have been, but I keep expecting it to change."

"Just watch out for those lead ankle weights," he warned her.

"Thanks."

But once again, and to her relief, the girls weren't at afternoon practice. In a way, this whole thing had worked out to her benefit. As a result of being "Queenie," as coach continued to call her, she'd probably gotten in better swims, better coaching, and the beginning of some better friendships with the guys. She remembered the Bible verse about everything working together for good when you served the Lord. Maybe that was happening here.

Although, she wasn't feeling quite as confident at the football game. She and Conner had just gotten seated in the bleachers when Haley and friends sat in the empty seat directly behind them. Now DJ was well aware that a little jostling, bumping, and physical contact were pretty much the norm at a sporting event like this, but it seemed that the girls behind them were taking it to a new level. Although they didn't seem to be taking any pokes at Conner, DJ noticed. But they were just in the second half of the game, and she'd gotten several sharp jabs in the back of her head, along with several knees in her back. Finally, she was getting really irritated.

She turned around to see Bethany sitting directly behind her—and smirking. "If you don't mind," said DJ as calmly as she could. "I'd appreciate it if you'd keep your knees to yourself."

Bethany gave her a mock innocent look. "Excu-use me, but it's a little crowded in the bleachers, if you haven't noticed."

Conner turned around now too. He actually smiled at Bethany, but DJ could see it was a stressed smile. "Just chill, will you, Bethany?"

She held up her hands and made another mock innocent look, and, realizing there was nothing else to do, DJ and Conner turned around.

"Maybe we should just move," suggested Conner, glancing around the crowded stadium for vacant seats. But it appeared to be standing room only now.

"No," said DJ firmly. "We have every right to be here without harassment." But even as she said the last word, she felt something icy wet and cold down her back. She jumped to her feet and shrieked.

"What?" said Conner.

DJ turned to face Bethany again. Bethany was feigning surprise and holding up her cup.

"You poured your soda down my back?" DJ exclaimed incredulously.

"It was an accident," claimed Bethany.

"Oh, yeah, right." DJ was still standing, trying to shake the sticky wetness and ice out of her coat and shirt.

The other girls laughed. "Just chill, DJ," said Amy. "Accidents happen, okay?"

"Yeah," said Bethany. "You don't have to freak. I'm sorry."

Haley just giggled with her hand over her mouth.

DJ sat down and looked at Conner. "I'm freezing now."

"Let's go." Conner turned and looked at the three girls with narrowed eyes. "I hope you're all proud of yourselves. Very mature."

And with that, Haley burst into tears.

DJ just shook her head, gathered up her purse, and headed down the bleachers. Too weird. Too freaking weird.

"I might have some dry clothes in my truck," offered Conner.

"I just want to go home," said DJ. She felt close to tears now too.

"What's up?" asked Taylor as she and Seth emerged from the stadium.

DJ rolled her eyes. "Bethany Bruiser couldn't keep her hands off of me, and when I confronted her, she poured her soda down my back."

Taylor laughed, and DJ scowled at her. "Sorry," said Taylor. "I mean, I'd be totally ticked if I were you, but you have to admit it's kinda funny."

"Real funny." DJ made a face. "I just want out of here."

"It's a boring game anyway," said Taylor. "We were leaving too."

"Yeah," said Seth. "Those Mighty Maroons are looking mighty wimpy tonight."

"Why don't you go change out of your wet stuff and meet us in town?" suggested Taylor.

DJ considered this, but the prospect of hanging with Taylor and Seth was a little scary, especially considering that DJ and Conner were still maintaining the "just friends" relationship.

"Thanks," she told Taylor. "But I think I'll call it an early night. I've got that meet in the morning."

Taylor shook her head. "Ever the devoted athlete."

The truth was DJ was relieved to call it a night. She didn't care if she was the only Carter House girl at home, she was glad to see her room. And even more glad to take a hot shower and get ready for bed. It was nice having the bedroom to herself. And once she got into bed, she opened her Bible, not to any place in particular. She simply allowed the pages to open and when she looked down, she instantly knew that this section was familiar. It was the fifth chapter of the book of Matthew. And her eyes stopped on a verse that she had read several times before. Unfortunately, it wasn't any easier to accept it this time. It was that verse about loving your enemies. About exchanging kind words for mean ones ... and doing something good in return for something mean ... and even praying for people who wanted to hurt you. Yowzers.

She closed the Bible and closed her eyes. "Okay, God, if you want me to do that, you are going to have to show me how. The last person I feel like loving right now is Bethany Bruiser. But if anyone can change my heart on this, I know it's you. Bring it. Amen." Then she turned off the light and hoped for better things.

"Way to go, DJ," said Coach Reynolds after she'd qualified for the final heat in freestyle. "I only expected you to swim today, but you're actually competing, and you're blowing me away, girl." He slapped her on the back now.

"Thanks!" she glanced over to where Haley and her gang were gathered in the bullpen waiting for their medley relay. DJ was so thankful that she wasn't part of their relay team. She hoped that never happened.

"You didn't tell us that you were actually good," said Taylor as DJ took a break with them.

"Oh, I don't think it's that I'm good, it's just that the competition is pretty lame."

"I think you're actually good," said Casey.

"I've got to get out of here for some fresh air," said Taylor. She patted her hair nervously. "And I hate to think of what all this humidity is doing to my do."

"You look gorgeous as usual," said DJ.

"And you look like a drowned rat," said Taylor as she picked up her bag. "Back in a few."

"Fresh air . . ." DJ shook her head. "We know she's just going out for a smoke."

"To each her own," said Casey. Then she nodded over to where Haley and her friends were getting set for the relay. "Any problems with Bruiser today?"

"Only if looks could kill."

"Doesn't she do freestyle too?" asked Casey.

"She and Haley both."

"Were their times better than yours?"

"I didn't check."

"Anyway, you looked good out there. Strong."

"Thanks. I'll just be glad when it's over."

But DJ was more than glad when it was over. She was flabbergasted. Not only did she swim her best time ever in freestyle, she beat Bruiser and took second place, right behind Haley. DJ had a feeling that if she worked a little harder she might be able to beat Haley next time. Not that she was out to beat Haley. If anything, she'd been going out of her way to be nice to Haley—as well as her friends. She'd congratulated them on winning the medley relay. Not that they'd even responded. Still, DJ was trying to take that Bible verse seriously.

DJ wasn't surprised that Haley and her friends were freezing her out in the locker room. But she was surprised to see that some of the other swim team girls seemed to be getting tired of the game. Several of them congratulated DJ on her times, and Monica Bradshaw even came over to dress with her.

"This thing with Haley is getting old," she told DJ. "The sooner she moves on the better it will be for everyone."

DJ nodded as she zipped her jeans. "I couldn't agree more."

"I'll tell you one thing," said Monica. "I've had it with morning practices. I'm coming back to afternoons starting Monday."

"Me too," said a short, brown-haired girl named Daisy. "Getting up in the dark is for the birds." She laughed. "Actually, I don't even think the birds like it."

And so, as DJ gathered up her things and left, she felt just a tiny bit hopeful, like maybe things were about to change.

"Don't think that this is over," said Bethany as DJ exited the locker room. Then she grabbed DJ by the arm and looked her straight in the eyes in a frightening way. The foyer to the pool was strangely vacant, and DJ glanced nervously around to see if she could spot anyone.

DJ took in a quick breath and shot up a prayer. "Look, Bethany, I really don't see why you're—"

Bethany shook DJ by the arm now, narrowing her eyes. "I didn't ask for your opinion—"

"Hey," said Taylor in that smooth husky voice of hers. "What's going on here, girls?"

"Yeah," said Casey behind her. "What's up?"

Bethany released DJ with a shove, still glaring at her. "If you think your Barbie doll friends are going to be any help, you might want to think again, DJ." Then Bethany turned to

Taylor and Casey and actually sneered. DJ almost expected her to snarl as well.

Taylor actually laughed. "You really need to get a life, girl-friend, and stop watching so much of those dramatic TV series."

"And keep your hands off DJ," added Casey.

"Yeah, right." Bethany stormed back to the locker room now ... probably to report to her friends.

"What a loser," said Casey.

"And a bowzer," added Taylor. "Seriously, that girl looks like she needs professional help, and I'm not just talking mental either."

DJ took in a deep breath and slowly let it out. "She's obviously not a happy camper."

"Do you think she was going to beat you up?" asked Casey.

DJ considered this. "I don't really know."

"Were you scared?" asked Taylor in a slightly mocking way.

"I sort of was," admitted DJ. "Anyway, I'm glad you guys popped in when you did. Thanks."

"Well, enough chit-chat," said Taylor. "It's time to shop till we drop!"

"Or our credit cards flop," added DJ.

11

viva vermont!

"SHOULD WE HAVE INVITED Rhiannon to come with us?" asked DJ as she was driving toward the city.

"I did ask her," said Casey. "But she and Bradford already had plans."

"And Eliza and Kriti are doing their shopping in *Manhattan*." The way Taylor said this almost sounded like envy.

"And they didn't invite you along?" teased DJ.

"Yeah, like *that's* going to happen."

"I thought you and Eliza were getting along better."

"Eliza and I are like oil and vinegar," stated Taylor.

"How's that?"

"Occasionally we go together, but we basically don't mix."

"Turn here," said Casey.

"I thought we were going to the mall," said Taylor.

"We're going someplace else first," said Casey.

"Someplace else?" Taylor didn't sound convinced.

"We're going to check out the sports shops at the factory outlet mall."

"Factory outlet mall?" Taylor wrinkled up her nose as if Casey had suggested they were going shopping at the local garbage dump. "Are you serious?"

"As a matter of fact I am," said Casey.

"Do you know what a factory outlet mall is?"

"Yes. It's a place where you get a good deal."

"It's a good deal if you want damaged, outdated junk."

"It's not like that," protested Casey.

"It can't hurt to try," said DJ. Even though Grandmother had given her a fairly comfortable budget for shopping today, DJ was hoping not to spend it all on ski clothes. The idea of saving a few bucks appealed to her.

"Why don't we just go to a real mall," complained Taylor. "It's already past two o'clock, and we'll just be wasting precious shopping time."

"Trust me, Taylor," persisted Casey. "This outlet mall has good snowboarding stuff. There's a North Face and Columbia and—"

"Yeah, yeah," said Taylor. "Whatever . . . shanghaied while shopping . . . well, it just figures."

As it turned out, Casey's idea to shop the factory outlet was very smart. After a couple of hours, all three girls had discovered some great finds and great prices as well.

"Check out these Chanel shades," said Taylor as they met at the car to stow some bags in DJ's trunk. She struck a pose to show off her new sunglasses. "Cool, huh?"

"And did you see the North Face jacket I got?" asked Casey as she tugged a bright yellow parka out of a bag and proudly held it up.

"The color's a little bold, but the style's not bad," said Taylor. "But look at this Nils." She pulled out a chic brown jacket with a fur-trimmed collar.

"Is that real fur?" asked DJ.

"Oh, yeah." Taylor rubbed it over her face. "Cool, huh?"

"Cool if you like wearing a dead animal around your neck," said Casey. She was probably still feeling tweaked over the color comment.

"Yeah, whatever." Taylor pointed to Casey's leather boots. "You're wearing cows on your feet."

Casey cracked a smile now. "Okay, I'm probably just jealous, Taylor. That's a totally cool jacket."

"What'd you find, DJ?" asked Taylor, eyeing her oversized shopping bag.

"I hit Columbia Outfitters," said DJ. She pulled out the light-blue jacket and a pair of denim-blue pants. Both items were top rated for warmth and comfort — ready to hit the slopes. Now DJ just hoped that her leg would be ready too. Right now, it was starting to feel sore, which she knew was probably a result of the swim meet and walking around on all this pavement.

"Okay," said Taylor. "I think that's all the damage I can do in this little mall. How about if we hit the real mall now?"

So DJ drove them over to the "real mall." But after about an hour of walking around — make that trailing Taylor around — DJ begged off to take a break. "My leg is starting to really ache," she told them. "How about if I hang at the food court until you two finally drop?"

"Works for me," said Casey, who had gotten surprisingly into this whole shopping thing. In fact, it seemed she and Taylor were getting along better than ever lately. Something DJ knew she should appreciate — wasn't it better than fighting? Still, she couldn't help but feel concerned for Casey's sake. Taylor wasn't exactly the most wholesome influence. DJ and Rhiannon had both been praying for Casey, and sharing their faith with her, and hoping that she'd start to figure things out again. Linking with Taylor could be a real setback.

"I only need about an hour more," said Taylor.

"But keep your phone on," said Casey. "We'll call you if we get waylaid."

"Here," said Taylor, handing DJ a bulky fashion magazine that she'd picked up along the way. "If you get bored, you can read this—maybe even learn a thing or two about fashion."

DJ rolled her eyes. "Yeah, right."

Even so, she was relieved to get away from them. She bought a slice of cheese pizza and a soda, found a vacant table off in a quiet corner, and sat down to relax. Sore leg or not, DJ didn't think she'd ever be as into shopping as Taylor and Eliza—and now, apparently, Casey too.

DJ finished her pizza and sat sipping on her soda and people watching and looking at the Christmas decorations—wasn't it just Halloween? Then she heard her phone ping. She picked it up thinking it was Taylor or Casey, but noticed it was a text message. DJ was not into texting. Oh, sure, she knew how. Who didn't? But she thought it was dumb, as did most of the girls at Carter House, well, except for Eliza and Kriti. They still did it sometimes. But DJ had always thought it was dumb. If you wanted to talk to someone, why not just call them like a normal person?

Still, she was curious. Who would be texting her? But as she read the message, which seemed more like a threat than a greeting, she realized it was anonymous. How was that even possible? She read the message again, more carefully this time, making sure that she'd decoded it correctly. But it seemed clear. The message said, ULL B SS CLAB S NO1 S 4 U, which loosely meant, "You'll be so sorry, crying like a baby sorry, no one sorry for you."

"Real nice," she said as she set the phone aside. It was bad enough to send a mean text, but to do it anonymously? That seemed pretty lowdown and cowardly. Still, it didn't take a genius to figure it out. It had probably been sent from one of Haley's friends. Or maybe even Haley herself. Although DJ didn't think that Haley would actually stoop that low. Especially when DJ recalled how Haley had been genuinely nice originally, reaching out to DJ when DJ needed a friend. No, it was probably the work of stupid Bethany. Still, it was irritating.

In an effort not to obsess over the stupid message, DJ opened Taylor's fashion magazine and absently flipped through the pages. She was actually trying to focus on the glossy photos of the "fashionable" stick-thin models, all airbrushed and perfected—totally unreal. Yet all she could think about was poor, stupid Bethany. So, instead of seeing Kate Moss's face, DJ was seeing Bethany's small eyes, fat ruddy cheeks, and bad complexion.

Talk about freaky. DJ slammed the magazine closed and shook her head. Why was she letting that stupid girl get to her? Seriously, Bethany was not worth the time. Even so, DJ read the message again, hoping she'd misunderstood, or perhaps imagined it. But it was still there—just exactly as she remembered it.

"Hey," said Taylor, making DJ jump.

"Oh!" DJ looked up at Casey and Taylor with wide eyes.

"What's wrong?" asked Casey.

"Yeah, you look like you've seen a ghost," said Taylor as she pulled out a chair and sat beside her.

"I just got this text message, and I guess it was weirding me out."

"Text messages are so lame," said Taylor.

"Let me see," said Casey.

DJ wasn't sure she wanted anyone to see it. In a way, it was kind of embarrassing. "Oh, it's nothing."

"Come on," urged Casey. "If you're weirded out, you should let us in on it. Maybe we can help."

"Yeah," said Taylor. "Who sent it?"

"That's just it," said DJ. "It was anonymous."

"Anonymous?" Taylor frowned. "How's that even possible?"

"Exactly what I was wondering. Isn't that illegal?"

"No," said Casey. She took the phone out of DJ's hand now. "There are ways to set up an anonymous text."

"You *would* know that," said Taylor in a disgusted tone.

DJ knew that Taylor was remembering what Casey had done on MySpace.com. Sometimes too much technology knowledge was dangerous.

"Wow," said Casey. "Someone is out to get you, DJ."

"Ya think?" DJ rolled her eyes.

"What's it say?" asked Taylor.

"Just that girls like DJ would be sorry, and no one would be sorry for them," said Casey.

"That sounds like a threat," said Taylor.

"Yeah," agreed Casey. "And no mystery about who sent it."

"I'm thinking Bethany," admitted DJ. "But I suppose it could've been Amy or Haley."

"That doesn't really seem like Haley's style," said Taylor.

"That's what I thought too."

"But it's because of Haley," pointed out Casey. "I can't believe she's not over the whole thing with Conner yet. Talk about obsessive."

"Well, don't let it get to you," said Taylor.

"You don't think I should be worried then?" DJ frowned down at her phone.

"I don't see why," said Taylor. "They're just trying to rattle you. The best thing is to pretend like you don't care. They get satisfaction if they think they're getting to you."

"You sound like you know a lot about this," said Casey.

Taylor narrowed her eyes. "Well, as you should know, I've had my share of enemies, Casey."

Casey glanced away uncomfortably.

"But, lucky for you, I don't hold a grudge," added Taylor.

Even as she said this, DJ couldn't help but think about the Bible verse she'd read just last night ... about loving her enemies. And DJ remembered her prayer and her hopefulness that God was going to help her love these obnoxious girls. But after Bethany's hostile confrontation and now this stupid text message, DJ felt anything but loving.

"Hey," said Casey. "You want me to anonymously text Haley or Bethany back—telling them to bug off?"

"Casey," said Taylor with impatience. "Weren't you listening to me?"

"What?" Casey frowned.

"If you play their game, they will simply think they are winning."

"Oh, yeah ... right."

"How do you know how to do this kind of thing, anyway?" asked DJ, holding her phone up. "Do you send anonymous texts to your enemies?"

Casey smiled sheepishly. "I refuse to answer on the grounds that it might incriminate—"

"Yeah, yeah," said Taylor. "Spare us the details."

"Well, I don't do it anymore."

"But how did you learn to do it in the first place?" persisted DJ.

"Like everyone else. Online. You can learn anything online."

"Yes," agreed Taylor. "Whether it's making an atomic bomb or how to cook your own crack cocaine, just go online and it's all there."

"That's right," said Casey. "And so is the FBI. You link up with some of those websites, and you'll have a pair of suits knocking on your door."

"You know this from experience?" asked Taylor with a slightly concerned expression.

"No." Casey grinned. "But I do watch TV."

"Sometimes you scare me, Casey." DJ just shook her head. Then, as a distraction from her stupid text threat, DJ pointed to their bags. "What'd you guys get anyway?"

Now Casey looked slightly uneasy. "Oh, nothing ..."

"What do you mean, nothing?" demanded Taylor. "I thought what you got was pretty hot."

"Hot?" DJ frowned.

"Steamy," said Taylor with a sly grin.

DJ looked back at Casey. "And it's for the ski weekend?"

Casey just shrugged. "Yeah ... whatever."

Taylor was opening her own bag now. It was obviously from the same shop. Then she unfolded the pale pink tissue, removing a black, lace-trimmed camisole and then a pair of matching bikini panties. "Cute, huh?"

DJ frowned. "Is *that* for the ski weekend?"

Taylor nodded smugly.

"Doesn't look very warm to me."

Taylor laughed her low, husky laugh. "Oh, there's more than one way to keep warm on a cold winter's night."

DJ peered at Casey now. "Please, don't tell me you got the same thing."

"Well, she didn't get the same color," said Taylor defensively. "That would be pretty tacky."

"Tacky." DJ just shook her head. Yeah, that pretty much summed it up for her.

Taylor carefully wrapped up her skanky garments in the tissue paper, seemingly oblivious to whether anyone was watching her. Then she slipped the bundle back into her bag with a satisfied smile. Casey just sat there and said nothing.

Okay, DJ knew she was about to be a spoilsport in both of their eyes. But she couldn't help herself. "Tell me you two aren't going up to General Harding's lodge with plans for having some big orgy."

Taylor laughed. "An orgy? Puleeze, DJ, get serious."

"You know what I mean." DJ narrowed her eyes at Taylor. "There's only one reason you're buying something like that."

"Because I like pretty things?" said Taylor innocently.

"You know that's not what I'm saying. You and Casey are plotting some stupid skanky plan for the weekend, and I just want to tell you that I think it's totally wrong and dumb and—"

"I'm just being a good Girl Scout," said Taylor lightly.

"Huh?" DJ felt derailed.

"You know the old Girl Scout motto: Be prepared for anything."

Casey snickered, and DJ felt like screaming. What was wrong with these girls? Instead, she picked up her bag and fished out her keys.

"I'm tired," she told them as she stood up. "I'm going home. If you want a ride, you better behave yourselves."

12

viva vermont!

BY WEDNESDAY OF THE FOLLOWING week, DJ had received thirty-seven anonymous text messages—not that she was counting exactly—each one sounding more hateful and threatening than the previous one. It was starting to get disturbing.

"Taylor said if I ignored them, it would stop," she told Conner as they sat waiting for their order at the Hammerhead.

"I think you should tell the police," he said solemnly.

"Seriously?"

"Yeah ... it's wrong for them to do this to you, DJ. And I'm sure it's illegal."

"But who would I accuse? The messages are anonymous."

"I don't think you have to accuse anyone. You just let them know what's going down, and maybe they can figure it out."

"You don't think that's like making a mountain out of a molehill?"

"I just think it's going too far." Conner looked seriously concerned now. "And it's making me remember something."

"What?"

"Well, Haley told me that she'd been treated for this thing. I can't remember what she called it—some initials—but it had to do with an inability to let things go. Kind of like she obsesses over stuff. You know?"

"Obsessive-compulsive disorder?"

"Yeah. That's it. OCD."

"Haley has that?"

He nodded. "I wouldn't even tell you, but what if she's behind this?"

"But Bethany seems to be the one—"

"Bethany is just doing Haley's dirty work."

"But why?"

He held up his hands. "Good question. Probably because Bethany feels honored to be Haley's friend. I mean, look at them—can you imagine a more unlikely pair?"

DJ considered this. "So Haley actually told you she had OCD?"

"She trusted me." Conner frowned.

"That probably makes you feel even worse now ..."

"Yeah, pretty much."

"Well, it's not like you would've told anyone ... I mean, if this hadn't happened. In a way she's asked for it. Not that I'll tell anyone else ... I mean, what would be the point?" DJ folded the napkin in half. "So did she say how having OCD affects her? Like why did she need to get help?"

"For one thing she struggles with anorexia." Conner sighed. "She thinks she needs to keep her weight down for diving and gymnastics."

"She's already tiny," DJ pointed out. "I can't imagine why she'd be concerned about her weight."

"Exactly. She obsesses."

"Oh ..."

"And she's this real perfectionist. Kind of a control freak, you know?"

"That's got to be hard."

"Oh, yeah . . ."

"And losing you, Conner. That was probably very frustrating for her. No wonder she's taking it so hard. I wish I'd known this."

"Why?" He looked slightly hurt now. "What would you have done differently?"

"I don't know," she admitted. "I mean, it's not like we're doing anything wrong. I mean, we're just friends. And anyone who's paying attention should realize that."

He nodded. "You'd think so."

"But back to your suggestion . . . do you really think I should call the police?"

"I don't know, DJ. I guess I just want it to stop."

"Well, Taylor felt certain that if I ignored it, it would stop."

"But it hasn't."

"Well, maybe I need to give it more time. The texts have only been coming for less than a week. If I just let it go . . ." The truth was that DJ was suddenly feeling sorry for Haley. She'd had no idea that she struggled with something like that. No wonder she'd been so weird about everything.

"I guess it can't hurt," said Conner as their food came. "As long as you don't let it go too far."

"And watch my backside," she teased.

"Did you hear the good news?" asked Taylor later that evening.

"What good news?" DJ tugged on a pair of wooly socks then hopped into bed. It had been cold lately, and the forecast for the weekend was more snow in the higher elevations. Perfect for the ski trip.

"The general has offered to drive us all to Vermont in his motor home."

"He has a motor home?"

"Apparently, it was just delivered yesterday. He stopped by at dinnertime to show it off. It's huge—like forty feet long—and totally awesome with a big flat-screen TV, leather chairs and sofa, gorgeous kitchen with stainless-steel appliances, a full bathroom, and a bedroom with a king-sized bed with another flat-screen TV. Really swanky in a cheesy sort of way." Taylor rubbed moisturizer onto her face and neck, her regular nighttime beauty routine.

"And he's going to let us ride in it?"

"He called it the model-mobile. He was going on about how he was taking his harem of beautiful girls on a road trip."

"And Grandmother too, right?"

Taylor laughed. "Of course."

"Wow, that's really nice of him. I thought we were going to be taking the train."

"No way. The plan is to leave at three thirty on Friday after school. That way we'll be at his lodge in time for dinner, which is, by the way, being catered. Not bad, eh?"

"On Friday?" DJ sat up in bed. "I thought we were going early on Saturday morning."

"Not now. This will give us almost three full days of skiing and snowboarding. Pretty cool, huh?"

"But I can't go."

Taylor frowned. "What do you mean?"

"We have a swim meet on Friday afternoon."

"Well, ditch it."

"I can't."

"Sure you can. You just don't go."

"No, they're counting on me."

Taylor didn't look convinced. "I'm sure that Haley and her thugs will be totally brokenhearted if you don't show."

"That's not it."

"Well, what then?"

"The coach is counting on me. My times have gotten better this week."

"So?"

"So . . . and there's the team too."

"Oh, yeah, like Haley and Amy and the adorable Bethany Bruiser. You don't want to disappoint them."

"No. I've made some friends. Monica and Daisy and Kara. In fact, we've decided to do a relay team together. But without me, they can't. It feels like I've just started to make some headway. If I don't go—"

"I can't believe you'd choose the swim meet over the ski trip."

DJ sighed and leaned back into her pillow. This was a disaster. "Why can't the general wait until Saturday morning?" she said almost to herself.

"You can't have your cake and eat it too," said Taylor in her grumpy voice.

"What's that supposed to mean?"

"That wanting it both ways isn't fair to the rest of us," she snipped. "Come on, DJ. Get with the program. It's just a stupid swim meet."

"I can drive you up there," offered Conner at lunch on Thursday. DJ had just dumped on him about being bummed because she had to choose between the swim meet and the ski weekend.

"Really?"

"Sure. I was going to ride with Harry. He's going up right after school too. But I know that Garrison would gladly take my place. Bradford is driving too, but he's already got a full car."

"How many guys are going up there anyway?" asked DJ.

"I don't know. You'd have to ask Harry. But the word leaked out, and my guess is there'll be at least a dozen of us. Harry told some of the guys to bring sleeping bags so they could crash on the floor."

"You really wouldn't mind taking me?"

He laughed. "What do you think?"

She thought she'd like to throw her arms around him and give him a great big kiss, but knew that it would be stupid not only because one of Haley's spies was probably watching, it would be breaking their pact to remain friends. So she just thanked him.

"How about if I come by your house tonight and pick up your stuff," he offered. "Then we can leave as soon as the meet ends tomorrow. Any idea when that'll be?"

She frowned. "Like around six?"

"Well, Harry said that it takes about three hours to get up there. So, even if we stop to get a bite, we should be there before ten. That's not too bad."

"Not bad at all." She grinned at him.

So it was set. She *could* have her cake and eat it too. She couldn't wait to inform Taylor.

"Any new text messages?" he asked in a lowered tone.

"Just two today." She sighed. "I deleted them without reading them."

"You sure that's wise? I mean, what if there was something specific?"

She shrugged. "It's more for my sanity's sake than anything."

"Well, just think," he told her. "You'll have three days in Vermont to put all that behind you. Maybe it'll blow over by the time we get back."

"Viva Vermont!" she said, and Conner echoed her. Naturally, several others at the table heard them, and now they were all laughing and lifting their soda cups as if to make a toast, yelling, "Viva Vermont!"

She rolled her eyes. "Look what we started."

"So, you decided to go then?" said Taylor as they were exiting the cafeteria.

DJ explained her plan with a happy grin. "See, I can have it both ways. You were wrong."

Taylor slapped her on the back. "Well, whatever, DJ. I'm just glad you won't be missing out."

"Me too."

Taylor held up her forefinger. "Although, you will be missing out on the general's motor home ride. Too bad."

"Yeah, whatever."

"You looked awesome today, DJ," said Monica as they got dressed after practice.

"Yeah," agreed Daisy. "Your leg of the medley was the fastest."

"Well, that's because I was doing the crawl," DJ admitted. "That's my best event."

"Well, your backstroke has really gotten better too," pointed out Kara.

"I think we have a chance to win the meet tomorrow," said Monica.

DJ nodded. More than ever she was thankful that she hadn't allowed Taylor or the others talk her into ditching the meet.

"Our relay team might even be good enough to beat Haley's," said Kara with confidence.

DJ frowned. "Well, even a second place wouldn't hurt."

"No, it wouldn't hurt," agreed Monica.

"But wouldn't you love to beat Haley?" asked Kara.

"Oh, I don't know …" DJ almost felt as if the locker room could be bugged. Sure, Haley and her friends were still doing morning practices, but who knew? "We need to remember that we're a team," she finally said. "We need to support each other."

"DJ's right," said Daisy.

"But a little healthy competition within the team is okay," said Kara hopefully. "Right?"

DJ grinned. "Right."

And DJ knew that Kara was right. But at the same time, DJ did not want to rock Haley's boat. It's not that she was afraid of her … more like she was concerned. Since Conner had told her about Haley's "little secret," DJ really had been praying for Haley. She hoped that at some point, she'd be able to talk to her and even invite her back to youth group.

When DJ got home, Conner's pickup was already there. "Am I too early to get your stuff for tomorrow?" he asked.

DJ slapped her forehead. "Oh, yeah, I nearly forgot."

"I don't mind waiting," he told her.

"Great." She led the way into the house. "Make yourself at home while I throw my stuff together."

"Then, if you want, we could sneak out for a burger."

DJ glanced around. That would make two nights in a row. Not that anyone was counting. Missing another low-cal, low-fat meal wasn't the least bit disturbing. "Sounds good," she told him. "I'll be down in a few minutes."

DJ raced up the stairs and began pulling out her ski clothes and stuffing them into her duffle bag.

"Is that how we pack?" asked Taylor as she emerged from the bathroom to discover DJ in a frenzy.

"That's how we pack when we're in a hurry," said DJ. "Conner's picking up my stuff so I can be ready to go tomorrow."

"You could just send your stuff with us," suggested Taylor, displaying once again just how smart she was. "The general's motor home has plenty of storage space. Don't you have a snowboard too?"

"He can take everything?"

Taylor smiled smugly. "That's what I'm saying."

"Cool." DJ dropped her duffle bag onto the floor. "In that case, I'm grabbing a burger with Conner."

Taylor looked slightly jealous now. Or maybe she was simply hungry. "I guess there are some perks to all your athletic obsessions."

DJ nodded, but just hearing the word *obsession* made her think of Haley. And that made her feel bad.

"Want me to express your regrets to your grandmother for not dining with the rest of us?" offered Taylor.

"Sure." DJ smiled. "Thanks!" Of course, as DJ dashed back down the stairs, she had to wonder why Taylor was so nice to her sometimes. Well, nice for Taylor anyway. Anyone else would probably consider that to be normal.

13

viva vermont!

DJ AND CONNER HAD JUST STARTED to eat when the door to the diner swung open and Haley, Amy, and Bethany walked in.

"Oh, great," said DJ with a mouthful of cheeseburger. "This is like a déjà vu all over again."

"Huh?"

"Haley and friends."

"Just ignore them," said Conner.

DJ focused her attention on slowly opening a bottle of ketchup and dumping a neat little heap right next to her fries. Then she carefully replaced the lid and set it back by the napkin holder. From the corner of her eye she could see the girls taking a booth near the front of the diner.

"Looks like they're not going to make an attack," said DJ.

"See," he told her. "Maybe it is going to blow over."

"One can only hope."

Even so, DJ and Conner took their time eating. The plan was to wait for Haley and friends to leave first. That way they could avoid any confrontations.

"You all ready for the big meet tomorrow?" asked Conner.

"I'm actually looking forward to it."

"Cool."

"I know. If anyone had told me last summer that I'd be swimming on swim team this year, I'd have told them they were nuts. But here I am doing it . . . and enjoying it too." Then she told him about her swim team friends Monica, Daisy, and Kara.

"Yeah, I've known Monica for years. She's okay."

"Kara seems kind of intent on beating Haley," admitted DJ. "But I reminded her that we're supposed to be a team." Then she told Conner how she'd really been praying for Haley. "I'd like to invite her back to youth group . . . you know . . . when it feels right."

"That'd be cool."

"She really does seem unhappy," said DJ, glancing up just in time to see Haley's little pixie face looking their way with a sad sort of longing. Of course, she then quickly looked away.

"I was thinking that this whole experience might actually be good for her," said Conner.

"How's that?"

"Well, sooner or later, she has to accept that she can't control every detail of her life."

"That's true," said DJ. "I've had to learn that one myself."

"So, let's just hope for the best."

DJ nodded. "And pray that God will get hold of her heart."

He gave her a thumbs-up. Then, to DJ's relief, the three girls finally left . . . with no confrontation. That seemed to suggest real progress. As Conner and DJ went out to the truck, she felt hopeful.

"Good luck," said Monica as she slapped hands with DJ. They were both in the holding pen for the backstroke event. So was

Haley, but as usual she was keeping her distance. When DJ attempted to give her what she hoped was an encouraging smile, Haley simply frowned and looked away.

DJ knew enough about sports and competition to know that some things had to be blocked out. And today she would have to block out Haley. Simply do your best, she told herself, and let the rest of it sort out later.

That's exactly what she did in the backstroke event — her best. And it just felt right. Oh, she had no idea which place she was in, but she knew she was swimming at her peak, and that felt good. But when she touched the edge of the pool and turned around, she was stunned to hear people cheering and clapping, and even more stunned to see that she had won that race. Haley had come in a close second.

Once she was deck side, she held out her hand to shake Haley's, almost expecting to be rejected, but to her surprise, Haley shook her hand. She gave DJ a small smile. Sure, it was forced, but it was better than nothing.

"Good race," said Haley quietly.

As the meet progressed, DJ thought that Haley shouldn't feel too badly since she was cleaning up in the diving competition. Not that there was much competition, since Haley was far and above the best diver.

But then it came time for the relays, and DJ could see that Haley and her friends were feeling nervous. In fact, DJ felt nervous too. But she tried to appear confident as she huddled with her relay team, each of them encouraging the others to do their best.

"Go for it!" said Kara. And then they went over to line up at the starting box. DJ made sure to keep her eyes on her own team, her own lane, and simply focus on her own swim — the last leg of the relay, and the same leg as Haley. She knew it was unlikely that her team would beat Haley's, but the truth was she hoped that they would. And why shouldn't she? She was an athlete. This was a competition. It was natural to want to win.

Her leg of the medley was, of course, crawl stroke, and she once again felt like everything was working, like she was giving this event her best effort and she would have no regrets. And, once again, she didn't allow herself to look into the other lanes, especially Haley's. She simply swam as if she were the only one in the pool, and going for her own personal record.

At the end, she looked up, and her teammates were all grinning and reaching down to pull her out of the water. Then they were slapping her on the back and announcing that they had just taken first place.

"That was awesome," said Kara.

DJ glanced over to where Haley's team was now helping her out of the water. "We really beat them?" DJ asked Kara quietly.

"Oh, yeah . . ." Kara nodded happily.

Haley looked unhappy as she toweled off her face, and DJ considered doing the handshake thing again. But due to the icy looks she was getting from Bethany, she decided it might not be such a good idea this time.

As it turned out, Crescent Cove High won the entire meet, and everyone on the team, or almost, was ecstatic.

"We've turned a corner," said Coach Reynolds as he gathered everyone for a little victory party, complete with snacks and some sparkling apple juice and plastic champagne glasses all ready to toast. "Here's to finishing the season strong."

DJ quickly lifted her glass, drinking to the toast. And just as quickly, she excused herself, hurrying to the locker room. It was already past six, and Conner was waiting on the sidelines.

She was eager to get on the road. She hurried to shower, dress, and partially dry her hair, managing to get out of there before the others began trickling in.

"Wow," said Conner. "That was quick."

She laughed as she threw her duffle into his cab. "Record breaking all around."

"Yeah, you were something out there, DJ. Really great meet."

"Thanks."

He grinned and started the engine. "And you don't look too bad in your swimsuit either."

She punched his arm playfully. "Thanks, I think."

"Did Haley say anything to you?"

"Not exactly. I mean, she said good race when I shook her hand, but it was kind of like she had to ... you know ... with people looking."

"Gotta be a good sport."

DJ sighed. "I actually felt kind of bad when I beat her in backstroke and then again in the relay."

"But kind of good too?"

"I guess. I don't mean the beating her part. Not really. But it did feel good to win."

"I think Haley kind of beat herself today."

"How's that?"

"Well, I was trying not to be too obvious, but I was watching her. She was really uptight. I mean, I've seen her at other meets, back when we were together, and she was more relaxed. More in charge, you know?"

"Yeah, I remember watching her with the team ... back when I was 'the handicapped girl' swimming laps in the handicapped lane, as Bethany called it."

"She said that?"

"Well, not until after you broke up with Haley and I became the number-one target on their hit list. Anyway, I do remember thinking that Haley was kind of like Queen of the Swim Team. Seriously, it was like she ruled."

"Now you're dethroning her."

"No, that's not true. She still rules in the diving pool. And she did take first in butterfly, if you were watching."

"But it's not the same, is it?"

"Is that bad?" asked DJ. "I mean, am I wrong to have joined the—"

"No, of course not. That's not what I'm saying. I actually think it's good for Haley to figure this stuff out. Obviously, she can't rule everything forever. She needs to learn to be a gracious loser."

"I guess . . ."

"Well, can you believe it?"

"What?"

"We're on our way to Vermont."

"Yay!" Now DJ's stomach growled. "But not until we get something to eat."

"I hear ya!"

The cab of the pickup was warm and cozy. After a big meal and a tiring day, DJ knew she couldn't keep her eyes open. "Do you mind if I take a little nap?" she asked Conner after they'd been on the road about an hour.

"Go ahead. It's a nice clear night . . . perfect for driving. We should be there just a little after ten."

"The general's motor home is probably already there now." She felt a slight twinge of envy as she considered how the other girls were traveling in such comfort and style. Still, she wouldn't have traded it for anything. Participating in the meet and getting to ride with Conner, well, that made up for luxury.

She settled her duffle bag like a pillow between them, curled up, and placed her head on top. Sure, it smelled like chlorine and was slightly damp from the pool, but in no time she was asleep.

DJ awoke suddenly. All was quiet, and Conner was gently tapping her on the shoulder. "Wake up."

"What?" She sat up and blinked in the darkness, trying to figure out where she was, and then realizing she was still in the pickup.

"Are we there?"

"No." Conner sounded slightly worried.

"Huh?"

"It's the pickup."

She frowned. "Out of gas?"

"No, I filled the tank in town."

"What then?"

"I'm not sure. But there was this loud noise and this grinding sound, and I knew I'd better stop before it got worse."

"You mean we're broken down?" DJ felt a small rush of fear. "Out here in the middle of nowhere?"

"That's what it looks like."

viva vermont!

"DO YOU Have any IDea what's wrong with the truck?" DJ asked in a small voice. "Like if you can fix it or not?" She knew that Conner was pretty mechanical. He and his dad had worked together to restore the pickup.

"I don't know. It was a pretty loud noise. Like something big might've broke. I'm surprised it didn't wake you."

"I was totally zonked." She glanced around now to see the outlines of trees in the darkness. They were in the wilderness. "Where are we anyway?"

"Well, based on the time, I'd guess we're about halfway to the lodge. Maybe better."

"Oh." She pulled out her cell phone. "Did you call anyone yet?"

"My phone's out of range. How about yours?"

She turned it on and waited, almost expecting to see another hateful text message. "Oh, it's out of range too."

Conner let out a loud sigh.

"What do we do?"

"For starters, I've got the emergency lights on. But I'll take a look under the hood too. Not that I think I can fix this. But you never know. Will you be warm enough?"

She shrugged. "I guess."

But as soon as he opened and then closed the door, she wished she'd brought her bags with her warm parka. She could use it now. She dug into her duffle to find a slightly damp hoody, which she wrapped around her shoulders. Not much, but better than nothing. While Conner poked around under the hood, a couple of cars drove past. She couldn't believe that they didn't stop to offer help. But then again, she knew if she was driving out on a dark country road, she probably wouldn't stop to help someone. Fortunately, Conner had a flashlight. That was something. Maybe he was getting it fixed. But after a while, he came back and got into the cab and rubbed his hands together.

"Man, it's cold out there."

"And in here too."

"It's a few degrees warmer in here," he pointed out. "But not for long."

Just then another car whipped past.

"You'd think someone would stop," he said. "I've got the hood up."

"Maybe we should get out where they can see us," she suggested. "So that they'll know we look harmless and in need of help."

"We could sit in the back with the flashlight," he said. "We could bundle up in some of my ski clothes."

"Let's go for it."

So they layered on some of Conner's things and climbed into the back of the pickup to wait for the next car. After what seemed like hours, DJ was getting worried. "What if no one else comes down this road?"

"I guess we could start walking ... but I don't know how far it is to the next town. The last one was too far to walk back."

"I see lights," said DJ hopefully. She stood in the back of the pickup and began to wave frantically as Conner held the flashlight to illuminate both of them. "Dear God," she cried out loud. "Please, send help now!"

"The car's slowing down," said Conner hopefully.

DJ was jumping up and down now, waving her hands and smiling. And, sure enough, an old station wagon pulled up behind them and an old man with long gray hair slowly climbed out.

"What are you kids doing out here in the middle of the night?" he demanded. Conner quickly filled him in about his truck and how their phones weren't working.

"Well, I can take you on to Everett Falls, but that's as far as I'll go and that's out of my way as it is."

"How far is that?" asked DJ.

"About fifteen miles."

"Is there a mechanic there?" asked Conner.

"There's a Shell station." The old guy frowned. "But it's getting late. Can't promise that they'll be open."

"But at least they'll have a phone," said DJ hopefully.

So they got into the old station wagon, which smelled like a herd of wet dogs had been riding in the back, and the old dude slowly—very slowly—drove them toward town.

"Got cataracts," he told them as he leaned forward to see out the windshield. "Can't see worth a darn at night. I wouldn't be out, except'n my dogs were outta food."

"I could drive for you," offered Conner.

The old guy laughed. "Not on your life, young man. You already destroyed one vehicle tonight. Don't ya think that's enough?"

Conner glanced nervously at DJ, and suddenly she wondered if they might've gotten into the car of a deranged psychotic or serial killer. She began to silently pray. If the clock on the dusty old dashboard was correct, it was already close to ten. Any hopes of making it to the lodge, even before midnight, were starting to fade.

Finally the lights of what appeared to be a very small town came into view, and DJ breathed a sigh of relief. Maybe this nightmare was about to end. But when the old guy dropped them out in front of a darkened gas station with no one around, she wasn't so sure.

"It looks closed to me," said Conner while the passenger door was still open.

"Just go knock on the door of the building next to it," their driver told them. "Hank should be there."

"Hank?"

"Hank's the one who owns the Shell station." Then, even before Conner could shut the door, the old guy stepped on the gas, pulling out so fast that his tires spit gravel and the passenger door slammed closed.

"Okay then ..." Conner tossed DJ a worried look. "I guess I'll just go and knock on the door."

"I'll go check out that café across the street," she said.

"I think it's a bar."

"Yeah, well, it looks like it's the only thing open, and maybe I can use the phone."

"Good idea."

Of course, as DJ went across the street, she wondered who she should call. It's not as if Grandmother could hop down here to get them. And no one else had a car.

"Hello," said a middle-aged woman as DJ entered the bar. She expected to be carded, but no one seemed to notice her age. Or maybe they didn't care. Well, it wasn't as if she was ordering a beer.

"Is there a phone?"

"Pay phone's back by the john," the woman told her.

This bar smelled musty and nasty and it got even worse back by the tiny hallway next to the bathroom. She wasn't even sure she wanted to touch the phone. Then she realized she would need some change.

"Can I get some change?" she asked the woman as she held out a twenty.

"Sure, if you buy a drink."

DJ considered this. "I'll have a Coke."

The woman frowned as she grabbed a none-too-clean-looking glass, put some ice in it, and then filled it with Coke. She thunked it down in front of DJ and then went to get her change. DJ waited impatiently. After the woman set her change on the table, DJ left a dollar behind. Maybe that would keep the bartender from asking for ID. A dollar tip for a Coke. Sheesh.

Back in the smelly hallway, DJ braced herself as she picked up the receiver and dropped a handful of change into the appropriate slots. She couldn't even remember if she'd actually used a pay phone before. Maybe back when she was in middle school and didn't have a cell phone. Or maybe she'd seen it in a movie. Anyway, she started to dial the numbers that she knew, beginning with Rhiannon's. But her phone was either turned off or out of range. Next DJ tried Casey's. But same thing. Finally, she decided to try Taylor's, and to DJ's surprise, Taylor answered with a groggy sounding "hey."

"Taylor, it's me, DJ," she said with relief. "Did I wake you?"

Taylor laughed. "Oh sure, like I was asleep. It's not even eleven. Where are you?"

So DJ quickly filled her in on the breakdown story.

"Well, that's too bad, but what do you want me to do?" Taylor's voice turned less than interested now. Almost as if DJ was disturbing her evening.

"I thought maybe you could give me one of the guy's numbers, and we could get him to—"

"I can do better than that," said Taylor. "I'm at Harry's place right now, and the guys are all here. Here you go."

"Hey, wha's up?" asked a slurred male voice.

"Who is this?"

"This is Harry, babe, who is this?"

"This is DJ. Are you drinking, Harry?"

"Not at the moment, but I think I've got one on the way."

"You sound wasted." She felt angry and disgusted. "Is there anyone there who hasn't been drinking?"

"Now what kind of party would that be?"

"How about Bradford?"

"Bradford ... Bradford? Hmm ..." There was a long pause with lots of background noise, and DJ began to wonder if Harry had set the phone down and forgotten all about her. She didn't know whether to hang up or just scream.

"No ..." he finally said. "Bradford and Rhiannon must've stepped out. Or maybe they weren't here in the first place. I really don't recall."

"DJ, this is Taylor again."

"What am I going to do?"

"I don't know. But I can tell you this. None of these guys are in good driving condition."

"What about the general?"

"Seriously, DJ. I'm sure he's gone to bed. Do you want me to go wake him and see if he—"

"No, no ..."

"Your grandmother's gone to bed too. That's how we sneaked out. There's no way I'm going to wake her. Not that she could help you. Just call a cab."

"A cab?"

"Yes. It might be pricey. But they can bring you up here, and you guys can figure out the mechanical things tomorrow."

DJ considered this. "I guess that makes sense."

"Of course it makes sense. Goodnight!"

DJ hung up and went back to the woman at the bar. At least the woman looked halfway friendly now. "Want another Coke?"

DJ shook her head. "No. I want a cab."

"A cab?" The woman threw back her head and laughed. "This girl thinks she can get a cab in Everett Falls."

The few patrons scattered around the bar laughed too.

The woman leaned forward and peered curiously at DJ. "Man, are you lost."

"We broke down on the highway," DJ explained. "We're on our way up to Ashton Peak for the weekend. If we can just get up there tonight, we could deal with the pickup tomorrow."

"That's all nice and good," said the woman, "but there ain't no cabs or taxis or buses here in Everett Falls." She glanced around the smoky room. "And even if one of these dudes offered to drive you up there, I wouldn't recommend it." She lowered her voice. "They're barely fit to make it home, and most of them are on foot, if you know what I mean."

"DJ," called Conner from the door. He was waving to her in a way that gave her hope.

"Hank is going to tow my truck into town, and he thinks he can get it fixed."

"No way!" She felt like cheering.

"Yeah. I'll go up with him. You might as well stay here." He peered around the room. "I mean, if you feel safe and everything."

She shrugged. "I'm fine. You get going."

So he took off, and she went back to the bar and sat on a stool across from the woman. "Do you have any coffee?" asked DJ.

The woman held up a glass pot filled with a dark thick liquid that looked like it had been sitting on the hotplate for several days, and DJ just nodded. Maybe she could doctor it up with cream and sugar.

"Was that your boyfriend?" asked the woman as she set the cup in front of her.

"My friend." DJ peered down at the muck in her cup and wondered if there was any way to make it drinkable. "Hank from the Shell station is going to tow his truck to town and—"

"Well, that's going to cost a pretty penny."

DJ nodded. "I guess. But it sounds like he's going to get it fixed, and we can make it on up to Ashton Peak."

The woman laughed. "Hank's going to stay up all night and work on your boyfriend's car?"

"Pickup."

"Car, pickup, bicycle ... whatever. But I just can't fathom Hank's gonna be out there working on it all night. Not the Hank I know."

"But that's what he told my—"

"Don't count on it, sweetie."

DJ frowned as the woman set a dish of creamers and sugar packets in front of her.

"I don't mean to pop your bubble. But Hank's just not that sort. I'm surprised he'd drag himself away from the TV to go out and tow anything this time of night. Your boyfriend must be paying him good."

"If that's true ..." DJ paused. "What will we do?"

"You mean for the night?"

"Yeah."

"I got a room I can rent. I don't usually rent by the night, but I could make an exception."

"A room?"

"Yeah. It ain't the Ritz. But it's not like you've got much choice in this one-horse town."

"No hotels?"

"No hotels, motels, guest houses ... sweetie, we don't even have a real brothel."

DJ rolled her eyes. Like they needed a brothel!

15

viva vermont!

"WELL, MAYBE YOU'RE WRONG about Hank," said DJ as she poured a second sugar packet into her coffee. "Maybe he'll get the pickup running tonight. And maybe we'll be out of your hair before long."

"And maybe pigs will fly you out of here too." The woman laughed loudly as she went to see if anyone needed a refill on their drink.

DJ sat and watched the grainy TV above the bar. An old rerun of *Law and Order* was playing, but at least it helped to pass the time. It was close to midnight when Conner finally reappeared.

"Bad news," he said as he pulled out a barstool and sat next to her.

"Hank's not going to fix the pickup?"

"How'd you know?"

She nodded over to the woman who was watching them as she lit a cigarette. "Small town," said DJ. "Word travels fast."

"Hank said it's the U joint, and that he'll get to it first thing in the morning."

"That's it then? We're stuck?"

Conner exhaled loudly then nodded. "That is unless you had any luck with the guys already up there. Any chance that Harry wants to make a moonlight run to get us?"

She quickly filled him in on the inebriated state of Harry and friends. "Even Taylor said it was a bad idea."

Conner glanced around the room as if hoping that a taxi driver might rise up from one of the tables. "And Hank said there are no buses or anything from here."

"That's what I hear." DJ shook her head. "What're we going to do?"

"I could call my dad to come get us. But by the time he makes it up here, it'll probably be close to two ... and Hank told me he gets up early. He thinks he could have the pickup running by nine. That means we could make it to the lodge before noon. Not that it would do much good since there's no place to stay. Hank told me there's no hotel. I guess I better just call Dad." He pressed his lips tightly together. "I'll probably get some big lecture too."

"Unless we take care of this ourselves." DJ sighed. "Apparently there's a room we could rent for the night."

"A room? As in one room?"

DJ held up her hands defensively. "It's not like I'm offering to sleep with you, Conner. I just mean there's a place where we can hole up until morning. Unless you'd rather sleep in your pickup." She brightened. "In that case, I'll take the room."

"I'd be a frozen corpse by morning." He shook his head. "I wish I'd brought a sleeping bag ... but Harry promised me a bed. Not that it's doing me much good now."

The woman, who must've been eavesdropping, approached them now. "You kids want to rent that room tonight?"

DJ glanced uncomfortably at Conner, and he just shrugged.

"I guess so," said DJ. "How much is it?"

"Well, like I said, it's not the Ritz. But then again, I don't normally rent it by the night either." She seemed to study them now. "But I'll let you have it for a hundred bucks. How's that sound?"

Well, it sounded like highway robbery, but DJ decided not to go there. Instead, she opened her purse.

"I can pay for it," said Conner.

"No," she insisted. "I'm paying. And you are sleeping on the floor."

The woman laughed as DJ counted out the cash. "Sleeping on the floor, now that's a good one." She handed DJ a brass key. "It's the second door on the left at the top of the stairs. The bathroom's down the hall."

"The bathroom's down the hall?" DJ whispered to Conner. "Meaning we share it with others?"

"I guess."

They went up the stairs without speaking, and DJ was feeling more and more uncomfortable with this. Really, what had she been thinking? On the other hand, what choice did they have? She put the key in the door and turned it.

"Want me to go in first?" he offered.

"Sure." The truth was she wasn't sure what to expect. But everything about this evening seemed to resemble a bad scene in some old horror movie. She expected to see a bloodthirsty ax murderer lurking around the next corner.

Conner flicked on the lights to reveal a stark room with tan walls and one window, a straight-backed chair, a dresser, and a full-sized bed with a bedside table and lamp next to it.

"It's not the Ritz," teased Conner.

DJ pulled back the coverlet to examine the sheets. Although they were yellowed, they seemed to be clean.

"Any bedbugs in there?"

"Yuck."

"Are you serious about me sleeping on the floor?" he asked as he looked down at the hard linoleum.

She opened a door to a tiny closet and found a spare blanket, which she handed to him.

"Gee, thanks."

She looked down at the floor now. It did look hard. And cold. "I don't know, Conner. This is a tough call. I mean, obviously, I don't think we'd do anything—you know—but, well, it just feels, you know . . ."

"Wrong." He nodded. "Yeah, I know. If you want me to sleep on the floor, I will."

She stood there considering everything and finally said. "No. Let's both sleep on the bed. But fully clothed, okay?"

He nodded. "Trust me, I was planning on sleeping fully clothed anyway, DJ. No way am I taking my clothes off in this place."

"And no touching."

He laughed. "Don't worry. I know the rules. We're just friends, DJ. We both agreed to that, right?"

She frowned as she stared at the bed. This was not how she'd planned to spend the night. Not how she planned to spend her first night with a guy. Not that that was what this was. She knew that. But at the same time it felt all wrong.

"I'm going to check out the bathroom," he said as he hung his jacket over the back of the chair.

"Let me know how it goes." Already DJ felt like she wanted to disinfect herself from everything she'd been exposed to in the bar—and normally she wasn't a real neat freak. Fortunately, she'd used the restroom when they'd had dinner. After a swim meet she was usually somewhat dehydrated and knew she could probably last until morning.

She peeled back the covers on the bed. After Conner's comment, she was checking for bedbugs now. Not seeing anything moving, she rolled the spare blanket into something of a barrier and laid it right down the center of the bed. Okay, she knew it was silly, but it made her feel better. Then she took off her shoes and climbed in and, lying down, she pulled up the covers and closed her eyes.

Eventually, she heard Conner return to the room. She had already decided to play opossum and pretend to be asleep. It seemed the simplest solution. She heard the bed creak and felt him carefully getting in beside her. He turned out the light and before long, she heard the even sound of his breathing and was pretty sure he'd fallen asleep.

As tired as she was, she was wide awake. But at the same time, she didn't want to move, didn't want to disturb him. Okay, on the weirdness scale of one to ten, this had to rank right up there at eleven. The craziness of the whole thing almost made her laugh. But she knew that might wake up Conner. And then she'd have to explain. Why risk it. Because despite all this lofty talk of just being friends and a purely platonic relationship, she still remembered what it felt like when he kissed her, when his arms were around her. In fact, she almost found it hard to believe that he was able to go to sleep like that. It seemed unfair.

That's when she knew it was time to pray. Here she'd been so worried about how he might act in this situation, and she was the one ready to jump all over him. Well, if that wasn't humbling. So she actually confessed this to God and asked him to help her stay in control of these reckless feelings. Finally, she asked God to help them get the pickup running and safely up to the lodge in the morning. Praying did the trick, because before long she was falling asleep too.

"Want to get some breakfast?"

"Huh?" DJ blinked at the light coming through a window.

"It's nearly eight," Conner told her. "I let you sleep in."

She sat up and looked around, attempting to get her bearings.

"Hank's working on the pickup. He thinks it'll be ready to go in about forty more minutes."

"Really?" DJ swung her feet around the bed and began putting on her shoes.

"Hey, did you know you snore?"

"So I've been told," said DJ.

"It's kind of cute, really. Kind of a puppy-dog snore."

"Gee, thanks."

"So how do you feel?"

"How do I feel?"

"I mean the morning after."

She turned and stared at him with shock. "What?"

"You know, after our first night sleeping together." He had a teasing grin, and she knew he was just jerking her chain.

She picked up her pillow and began smacking him in the head with it, over and over. "I feel just fine, Conner," she said. "How about you? How are you feeling?" She suppressed laughter as he tried to defend himself.

"Okay, okay!" He finally grabbed the pillow and tossed it to the bed. "Sorry. I thought you could take a joke."

She narrowed her eyes and then shook her head. "Not before breakfast, I can't."

"Let's get moving then. There's a tiny café down the street. Hank said the food's not bad." Conner laughed. "Not that we have any other choice."

As it turned out, the food wasn't bad. And the coffee, though not great, was way better than the bar's coffee last night.

"So, did you have sweet dreams last night?" Conner asked in a teasing tone after the waitress refilled their coffee cups.

"Are you nuts? I felt like I was starring in a Stephen King flick."

He chuckled. "Me too."

"Well, today should be much better."

He glanced at his watch. "Just think, we might be riding down the mountain in a few hours."

He wasn't far from wrong. A few hours—and a few hundred dollars—later, Conner's pickup was pulling up in front of General Harding's lodge.

"Wow, this is nice," said DJ as she grabbed her duffle. Hopefully, the girls had taken her other things inside by now, although she wouldn't be surprised if they'd forgotten. She just hoped that Taylor had remembered to mention this whole thing to Grandmother this morning.

"I'm heading over to Harry's," said Conner. "My guess is that the rest of them have already headed up the mountain by now. Want me to come back by here to get you?"

"Yeah, sounds good." DJ opened one of the big double doors and went into the spacious room. The floors in the entry were slate, and the big open beams looked like real logs.

"Well, well . . ." said Grandmother as DJ wandered into an open room with an enormous rock fireplace that went clear up to the high, vaulted ceiling. "You made it after all." Grandmother had on a stylish-looking ski outfit that probably wasn't going anywhere near the slope. She was comfortably seated in an overstuffed chair next to the crackling fireplace, with a mug of something hot and several magazines at her elbow.

"Did Taylor tell you about Conner's pickup breaking down?"

"Yes, which only proves that you should've come with us in the first place, Desiree. We had such a lovely ride up here."

"Well, that would've meant skipping out on the swim meet, Grandmother." DJ smiled at her. "And you've said that young ladies honor their word."

"That's true. Anyway, you are here now. In one piece. The others have gone up to the mountain. I was enjoying the quietness of this lovely place."

DJ sensed that was a hint to make herself scarce. "Do you know where I'm supposed to be staying?"

"One of the rooms on the second floor. I'm sure you'll find it if you look around."

DJ wasn't so sure, but decided to give it her best shot. She found a room with two beds, where it looked like Eliza and Kriti must be staying. Another nice suite at the end of the hallway appeared to be where Grandmother had made herself at home. Eventually, DJ found a large room with three sets of bunks, with her own things piled on one of them. *Voila!*

Relieved to be back in "civilization," DJ took a long hot shower, changed into her snowboarding stuff, and hoped that her snowboard would be somewhere easy to find outside. She'd also taken the time to put on the sturdy elastic leg brace that her therapist had insisted she wear for snowboarding. It felt a little awkward as she went down the stairs, but if it prevented any further injury it would be worth it.

"You be careful up there," the therapist had warned her. "Your leg is almost as good as new, but a hard fall could land you right back where you started."

"There you are," said Conner when DJ emerged. "Is this yours?" He held up the dark blue Burton board that her mom had gotten for her several years ago when DJ had insisted she had to go snowboarding or "die." Those were pretty much her words too. Now it was sadly ironic to think that it was her mother who had actually died. But DJ remembered how pleased her mom had been to present this board to DJ on her fourteenth birthday. "It's perfect," DJ had cried, throwing her arms around her mother. "How did you know?" Mom had teased her then, reminding DJ of how she'd left computer printouts and ads for this exact same board all over their condo.

"You okay?" asked Conner with concern.

"Yeah." DJ sighed. "Just remembering."

"Well, that's a cool board. Mine's a Burton too. You ready to hit the slopes?"

She grinned. "You bet. It's been a while, but I'm sure it'll all come back to me."

"We should probably get our boards waxed first," he said, nodding over to the big lodge. "And we need lift tickets and a map, since I haven't ridden here before. Have you?"

"Nope."

Fortunately, since they were late, the rush hour was over and they soon had everything they needed. "Did that guy say there were only four lifts?" asked DJ as they strapped on their boards and headed for a lift line.

"Yeah. This is a pretty small resort. But the good news is the lines are pretty small too."

Soon they were riding up the mountain and finally standing at the top and looking down.

"Viva Vermont!" said DJ and then she carefully took off. She'd already informed Conner that, because of her leg, she planned to take it slow and easy. "No kamikaze runs for this girl."

"Nice ride," said Conner when they regrouped at the foot of the hill. "For taking it easy, you go pretty fast."

"Thanks." She grinned. "Ready to go again—"

"Hey," yelled Taylor as she and Seth joined them. "The renegades have arrived."

"When'd you get here?" asked Seth as they all got into line together.

"About an hour ago," Conner told him.

Taylor grabbed DJ's hand now. "You're riding up with me, girlfriend."

DJ didn't argue. It was kind of nice that Taylor was glad to see her, but as soon as they were seated on the lift, Taylor started grilling her. Naturally, Taylor tried to make the night in a hotel sound like something it wasn't. But at least she was doing it with good humor.

"No, no," laughed DJ. "Nothing happened, I swear." Then, without thinking, DJ told Taylor about how she'd made a blanket bridge.

"You mean you slept in the same bed?" Taylor's eyes lit up.

DJ realized her mistake now. "Well, yeah, sort of. But we were stuck in this tiny town with no hotel. And there was just this one nasty little room, and I couldn't make Conner freeze in his pickup. Trust me, Taylor, we slept with our clothes on, and nothing whatsoever happened."

Taylor was laughing really hard now. "Yeah, sure, whatever you say."

"Honest! Nothing happened!"

Taylor nodded. "Lighten up, DJ."

"Huh?"

"I believe you. That's why this is so funny."

They were at the top now, and it was time to get off. "It's so funny."

"What are you saying?" demanded DJ as she adjusted her goggles.

"It's funny because only you, DJ, could sleep in the same bed with your boyfriend for an entire night and *not* have sex."

"Shh!" DJ glanced over her shoulder, worried that someone might be listening.

"Don't worry," said Taylor as she got ready to take off down the hill. "The trees aren't talking."

16

viva vermont!

IT FELT SO GOOD TO ride. DJ spread her arms as she imagined herself flying down the slope. She felt free like a bird and strong again. Yet she knew she needed to be careful. The last thing she needed was to hurt her leg again. As a result, she encouraged Conner to go his own way and hang with the more experienced riders, which was a group of mostly guys plus Taylor and Casey. Okay, DJ felt slightly envious because she knew, without her bad leg, she'd have not only kept up but could've possibly led the pack. Still, there was no point in moping. Besides, she was having fun.

"It's really nice of you to hang with me," said Rhiannon as they rode up the beginner hill together for about the sixth time. "You're a good coach."

"And you're really improving," said DJ.

"Thanks to you."

"Maybe you'll be ready to try the intermediate hill next."

"Yeah ... maybe ..."

But after Rhiannon did what looked like a painful faceplant at the foot of the easy hill, she was pretty rattled. "I'm sorry to slow you down," she said as DJ helped her up, brushing the snow off her face.

"It's okay," DJ assured her. "I really do need to take it easy. In fact, I think we both could use a break."

As they sipped cocoa in the main lodge, DJ asked about last night. "Sounded like a wild party going on," she said to Rhiannon. "But you guys weren't there? Where were you?"

"We were there for a while," admitted Rhiannon. "But it got too crazy. So Bradford walked me back to General Harding's lodge, and we just hung there. Isn't that a beautiful house!"

"Yeah." DJ nodded. "It's amazing. I can't believe he invited a wild bunch of girls up here to use it."

"Did you know that the art on the walls is real? And the sculptures are old and valuable. Bradford and I were checking it out. The general must be really wealthy."

"My grandmother said his family is one of the oldest and wealthiest in Connecticut."

"Do you think he and your grandmother would ever get married?"

DJ laughed. "It's hard to imagine. On the other hand, I know my grandmother is very attracted to money. Who knows?"

"Hey," said Casey as she joined them. "Are you two done for the day?"

"I think I am," admitted Rhiannon.

"I wouldn't mind another run or two."

"You guys go ahead," said Rhiannon. "I'll head back to the general's lodge and get a shower before it gets too busy."

"Good idea," said Casey. "Four of us are sharing one bathroom." She made a face. "Of course, Eliza and Kriti have their own."

"Of course . . ." DJ laughed.

"Oh, yeah," said Casey to Rhiannon. "Everyone is planning to come back up here after dinner. There's a band playing and stuff. Bradford asked me to let you know."

Then they went their separate ways, and soon DJ and Casey were riding up one of the more difficult runs. "Isn't it beautiful up here," said DJ as she looked out over the trees and snow and blue sky.

"Yeah ... pretty amazing."

"It's so good to get away." DJ took in a deep breath of cold fresh air.

"Speaking of getting away," said Casey. "I just remembered something."

"Huh?"

"Did you get any mean text messages yesterday?"

"Yeah, duh. I get them every day."

"What time of the day?"

DJ considered this. "Well, there are usually several at night, and a couple waiting for me in the morning. Naturally, I dump them. Then I turn my phone off at school. But by the end of the school day there are usually one or two more. Why?"

"Because I think I know who's doing it."

"Bethany, right?"

"Wrong."

"Huh?"

They were about to get off the lift now. "It's Haley."

DJ slid down, moving away from the lifts to wait for Casey to join her. "Haley?"

Casey nodded. "I noticed her in civics yesterday. Then I remembered she's usually at the computer at the end of each class—and I wondered why. So I looked over her shoulder in time to see she was on one of those sites."

"What sites?"

"The ones where you set up an anonymous account to text people."

"Seriously? She does it at school?"

"Apparently."

DJ shook her head. "That's so weird."

"Ready to rock and roll?" asked Casey as she zipped her coat up higher.

"You go ahead," said DJ. "I need to pace myself."

Casey whipped down the hill, and DJ paused to consider this. Haley was the one writing those mean messages. For some reason this seemed way more disturbing than if it was Bethany. DJ usually tried not to read the messages, but it was hard not to miss the gist of them. And some of the language and insinuations ... well, it was pretty nasty. She felt sad to think that Haley was full of such hate and anger.

"Focus on the ride," DJ told herself as she took off. "No more broken bones." Then DJ bent her knees and carefully glided down. When she got to the bottom, it had been a safe ride, but some of the fun seemed to be gone.

"You okay?" asked Casey.

"Yeah, I'm fine."

"You don't look fine." Casey frowned and peered at DJ.

"I just feel bad knowing that it's Haley."

Casey patted DJ on the shoulder. "Sorry. Guess I should've kept my mouth shut. Don't think about it, okay?"

"That might be easier said than done."

"Want to do another run?"

"Nah, maybe I should stop while I'm ahead."

"I'll join the others then," called Casey as she took off to where several of their friends were getting in a line for the most difficult run.

"Have fun," called DJ. "I'm heading back to the lodge."

Once again, the general had ordered a catered dinner. But the agreement was that the girls were in charge of cleanup. DJ thought that seemed a small price to pay, especially considering the caterers prepared real food and not the normal rabbit food the girls were used to having back at Carter House.

"This is the plan," said Eliza as the girls put things away in the kitchen. Eliza was sitting at the island, acting like she was the queen of the kitchen, but doing nothing. "We'll hang with the general and Mrs. Carter for a while — you know, play games or watch TV or whatever. Then we'll kind of trickle off to our rooms, saying how tired we are and whatnot."

"But don't be obvious," added Taylor. "Like if everyone starts yawning and making these stupid excuses —"

"Definitely," said Eliza. "Then we'll sneak off in pairs to go to the lodge."

"What if we don't want to?" countered DJ.

"Then don't," snipped Taylor. "Stay home with Grand-mother and knit."

DJ made a face. "I was just saying."

"Anyway, Kriti and I will go first."

"Why do you get to go first?" asked Taylor.

"Fine," snapped Eliza. "You go first, Taylor. Who's your partner?"

"Me," said Casey eagerly.

"So Casey and Taylor will lead the way. Just be quiet. Then Kriti and I will go, and last — and possibly least — Rhiannon and DJ can come, that is unless you guys want to be the goody-two-shoes of the group."

"I want to go," said Rhiannon. "The band is supposed to be good."

"I'll go too," said DJ. "But I don't see why we don't just tell them what we're doing."

"We don't want to worry them," said Eliza.

"Besides, this is more fun," added Taylor.

"And we all know where the key is hidden, right?"

"I don't," said DJ.

"Back door underneath the carved bear," said Taylor.

DJ felt a little guilty as she and Rhiannon finally slipped out the back door. Oh, she was pretty sure they wouldn't get caught since both her grandmother and the general had already turned in. But at the same time, DJ wondered if—as a Christian—she shouldn't be sneaking out. As they walked toward the main lodge, she mentioned this to Rhiannon.

"I kind of wondered that too," admitted Rhiannon. "Sometimes it's hard to know. I mean, no offense, but your grandmother ... well, she's not exactly a moral compass."

DJ laughed. "No, not exactly."

"But God is," said Rhiannon.

"So, what does God think of this?" asked DJ.

"Well, I know that God doesn't want me to drink," said Rhiannon. "But I sort of feel like it's okay to hang with our friends. Maybe I'm hoping that something we say or do will rub off, you know, like they'll see what we have and want to change."

"Like that night you talked to me at Harry's beach party?"

"Exactly."

"Right now I'm mostly worried about Casey."

"Me too."

DJ sighed. "She's really glomming onto Taylor lately."

"I've noticed."

"Talk about missing a moral compass."

"Tell me about it." Rhiannon pushed open the door to the lodge, and they began to hear the music.

"Anyway," said DJ. "It's nice hanging with you at times like this."

Of course, it wasn't long before Rhiannon was hanging more with Bradford, and naturally, Conner gravitated toward DJ. It's like everyone was pairing up. And this probably made sense because a lot of the couples were dancing. But, even so, it aggravated DJ.

It aggravated her even more when Conner put his arm around her. They'd gone out of the lounge to search out a soda machine and some fresh air. They'd been standing by the fire when he'd pulled that little stunt, and, naturally, she moved away and gave him a warning look.

"What's wrong?"

"You know," she hissed at him as she looked over her shoulder to see if anyone was watching. "We're just friends, remember?"

He laughed. "Not according to the rumors flying around the mountain today."

"What rumors?"

"The ones you started."

Now DJ remembered how her tongue had slipped with Taylor earlier.

"So everyone thinks we slept together last night." He winked at her in a teasing way.

"We did sleep together," she admitted. "But that was all, Conner. And that's exactly what I told Taylor. I made it perfectly clear."

"Well, that's not how Taylor's replaying it."

"Taylor is a well-known liar."

He nodded. "Yeah, but people still listen to her."

DJ let out a long sigh of exasperation. "You know what?"

"What?"

"I wish we were at youth group right now."

He kind of frowned. "Really? You don't like it up here?"

She considered this. "I do like it up here. But I don't like all these games. I don't like that we sneaked out of the house tonight."

"You sneaked out?"

"Yeah ... sort of."

He chuckled. "We just walked out."

"You guys don't have chaperones."

He frowned now. "Yeah, and I think some of the guys could use one."

"It bugs me that our friends are in the lounge right now—and they are using fake IDs to drink. I mean, isn't that illegal? Duh."

"Yeah. It bugs me too."

"I mean, other than you and me and Rhiannon and Bradford ... well, it's crazy. And that's why I'd rather be at youth group. At least we know where we stand there. Everything up here feels ... well, kind of slippery."

"Do you want to go home?" He studied her. "I mean, back to where you're staying?"

She nodded. "You know, Conner, I do."

"Let me go tell Bradford I'm walking you back."

But when he returned, both Bradford and Rhiannon were with him. They, too, were glad to get away from the whole bar scene.

"People get so stupid when they drink too much," said Bradford.

"Yeah," agreed Rhiannon. "I spent most of my life taking care of my mom while she was either drunk or high. I think I could use a break."

"It's too bad," said DJ. "Because they'd have more fun without the drinking."

"For sure," agreed Rhiannon. "You should've seen Taylor and Casey this morning. They were both pretty green around the gills."

"You guys should see Harry's cabin," said Bradford. "Or maybe not. It's pretty disgusting."

"And smelly," added Conner. "Last night's party must've been messed up."

"Will Harry just leave the place like that?"

"No way," said Conner. "He told me that housekeeping will come the day after we leave and put it all back to rights."

"What money can do," said Rhiannon sadly.

They were back at the general's lodge. "I wish we could invite you in," said DJ. "And it might be okay, but I'd feel better if I'd checked it out with the general first."

"Yeah," agreed Rhiannon. "It's such a nice place, Conner. I'm sure you'd like to see it."

"Maybe tomorrow," said DJ.

Then Rhiannon and Bradford kissed goodnight, and DJ stuck out her hand to shake Conner's. He shook it, but looked slightly disappointed.

"Goodnight, friend," she told him, waving as the two guys walked away. Then she found the hidden key and unlocked the door.

"Don't forget to put it back," Rhiannon reminded her.

DJ chuckled. "That'd be funny, huh?"

"Yeah, funny until they started pounding on the door."

"And I know that Grandmother is a sound sleeper and General Harding's hearing isn't so great."

"So we'd probably be the ones who'd have to get out of bed and go let them in."

"Although we could let them chill a bit first."

They both laughed, but then DJ did put the key back under the bear. For one thing, she knew she was too tired after last night to get up and let cranky and possibly drunken girls in after midnight. For another thing, she really didn't want to get up in the morning to find their frozen corpses on the back porch.

viva vermont!

"WHERE ARE THE OTHER GIRLS?" asked the general as he flipped a pancake. DJ and Rhiannon and Grandmother were the only ones at the breakfast table on Sunday morning, and Grandmother did not look pleased.

"They're sleeping in," said Rhiannon.

More like it sleeping it off, thought DJ. Casey and Taylor had both been totally wasted when they made their noisy entrance last night—make that early this morning. DJ was surprised that they hadn't woken up the general and her grandmother. Just a little while ago, DJ had stuck her head into Eliza and Kriti's room and was convinced that both of them had over-indulged as well. Kriti surprised DJ since she never used to drink. But, of course, Kriti was under Eliza's influence as much as anything else these days.

Really, DJ felt like things were getting more and more out of control, and she intended to have a talk with Grandmother. She just wasn't sure when. It almost seemed unfair to bring it up here at the general's place.

"Why not wait until we get back to Crescent Cove," suggested Rhiannon as they put the breakfast dishes into the dishwasher.

167

"You're probably right."

"Then you and I can speak to her together. I'll back you up."

DJ smiled. "That'd be great. I really want her to understand that it's serious. I mean, Taylor's parents might not care what she does, but I know that the other girls' parents would be furious if they knew what was going on."

"But, don't kid yourself, DJ. This could be going on even if they were at home. In Casey's case it was."

"Yeah ... I guess. Still, it seems wrong. And even more wrong to sit back and say nothing."

Rhiannon nodded. "Totally."

As it turned out, the guys, other than Conner and Bradford, weren't in very good shape either.

"That house is even more disgusting today," Conner told DJ as they rode a lift together. "Man, I don't see how even the best housekeepers can get it clean again. I won't go into details, but just imagine a dozen drunken guys sharing two and a half bathrooms. It ain't pretty."

DJ made a face. It sort of reminded her of the horrid "shared" bathroom back in Everett Falls. She had considered using it the morning after she and Conner had "slept together" but was so disgusted by the smell that she had waited until they went for breakfast at the café to relieve herself.

"Sorry," said Conner. "Guess I should spare you the details, huh?"

"Well, to be honest, it's no walk in the park sharing accommodations with Casey and Taylor either. One of them, I'm guessing it was Casey, must've gotten sick last night. She partially hit the toilet. But Rhiannon cleaned up the rest of it."

"It's too bad."

"Well, let's not think about it," said DJ as they got off the lift. "Let's not let those losers spoil our day."

He nodded as he pulled down his goggles. "That's right. Bad enough they're spoiling their own."

DJ glanced up at the gathering clouds overhead. "It looks like weather's coming. The best riding might be this morning."

"Viva Vermont!" he yelled as he shot down the slope ahead of her.

"Viva Vermont!" she cried even louder as she took off.

About midway down the slope she pulled over to the side and paused to take in the beauty all around her. Really, it was incredible up here—truly God's country. But it was too bad that some people were too blind—or too wasted—to even see it. Still, she was determined not to allow the stupidity of others ruin this day for her.

Rhiannon's skills seemed to be improving, and she finally felt brave enough to attempt one of the more difficult runs. "I'll stick with you," promised DJ at the top of the hill, "and the guys can go ahead if they want."

"We'll wait for you at Midway," said Bradford.

So Rhiannon and Casey enjoyed a slow, careful ride down, and Rhiannon only fell once. At Midway, they saw the guys sitting off to the side and joined them.

"Isn't it awesome up here!" said Bradford as Rhiannon flopped down next to him.

"Yeah, it makes me want to sing a praise song," said Rhiannon.

"Well, it is Sunday," said Conner. "Go for it."

So in her beautiful, clear voice, Rhiannon started a song that they all knew from church and youth group. And before long, they all joined in. Then she started another song, followed by another. DJ thought it was the most incredible thing she'd ever done. To sit up there in the pristine white snow and the tall pine trees, just singing songs to God—it almost made her want to cry, but with happiness. When Rhiannon finally ended the last song, they all just looked at each other in amazement.

"That was awesome," said DJ in a hushed voice.

"Kind of like being in church," added Conner.

"Only better," said Bradford.

"This is like church," said Rhiannon. "God said where two or more of us gather together he's in our midst."

"I can't imagine a more spectacular church," said DJ.

"Is it okay to pray?" asked Rhiannon in a quiet voice.

"Of course!" exclaimed Conner, and they all nodded.

"Dear God," began Rhiannon. "We just want to say how much we love you, and we want to thank you for this amazing time—and this incredible weekend. You are awesome, and we really do appreciate you."

"Yeah, God," continued Bradford. "We know we're not perfect, but we also know you're working on us. Help us to be a better source of life for our mixed-up friends. Help us to love them the way you would love them."

"That's right," said Conner. "Instead of wanting to kick some ... well, you know ... help us to say the right things to these guys. Help us to direct them to you. We believe you can do miracles—just like you've done in us."

DJ felt it was her turn, but she still wasn't totally comfortable praying with others. Even so, she took in a deep breath and began. "Dear God, I agree with everything these guys just said. I really do want to show your love—especially to Taylor and Casey. I worry about them, God. And I want them to come to you the way that I have—we have—come to you. Please, show us how to reach these guys for you—with your love."

Then they all said "amen!" This was followed by a group hug and a joyful ride down the rest of the hill. They got in several more rides before the snow started to fall. But by one o'clock, it wasn't looking too good.

"Why don't you guys come over to our place," suggested DJ. "I'm sure the general won't mind."

So they all trudged through the snow to the general's lodge, planted their snowboards by the back door, and went inside to see that the other girls were just starting to stir. They looked pretty awful, and when DJ started to pull things out of the fridge to make sandwiches for lunch, Kriti, who had just made a cup of tea, held her hand over her mouth and made a fast dash to the nearby powder room where they couldn't help but hear her emptying her stomach.

"Poor Kriti," said DJ as she set a jar of mayonnaise on the counter.

"I'll go check on her," offered Rhiannon.

DJ continued to put out stuff for sandwiches. Her plan was to create a sandwich bar and let everyone fend for themselves.

"Kriti is one sorry girl," said Rhiannon when she came back.

"Feeling pretty nasty?" asked Conner as he began to build his sandwich.

"Oh, yeah."

"Maybe it'll be a lesson for her," said Bradford.

"I hope so." Rhiannon reached for a plate. "She said she's never going to touch alcohol again."

"Here, here," said Conner as he held up a can of soda.

"Hey, maybe they'd like some Sierra Mist," said DJ. Then she grabbed a couple of cans and ran up to their room.

"What d'you want?" asked Taylor as she sat in a chair looking like something the dog had dragged in.

"I brought you a soda," said DJ as she set it on the desk.

Taylor brightened ever so slightly. "Thanks."

"Sorry you missed out on this morning."

"Oh … well … maybe later."

"There's a storm coming in now," DJ told her. "So I doubt you'll want to go up there until it breaks."

"Don't worry," said Taylor. "I don't think I want to go anywhere for a while."

Then DJ let herself into Eliza and Kriti's room. Poor Kriti was flopped out on her bed again, looking even worse than Taylor.

"You okay?" asked DJ.

Kriti waved a hand without speaking.

"I brought you a soda."

Kriti closed her eyes and muttered a weary "thanks."

DJ felt slightly hopeful as she returned to her friends in the kitchen. "Maybe this will put the brakes on all the crazy partying," she told them as they sat down to eat their lunch.

It snowed for the rest of the afternoon, but it was fun being stuck in the fabulous lodge with a crackling fire and all the other amenities. The four young people ended up playing charades and Pictionary with Grandmother and the general for a couple of hours. DJ was surprised to see this playful side of the general. Normally, he was somewhat formal and polite, as well as slightly intimidating with his perfect posture and steely gray hair. But during charades he cut loose and managed to crack them all up with his offbeat sense of humor. Really, by three in the afternoon, DJ felt like it was turning out to be a perfect day.

"How sweet that you're humoring the old folks," said Eliza as DJ returned to the kitchen to refill her coffee cup. By now the other girls were pretty much back to life. With showers, makeup, and fresh wardrobe, they could almost pass for healthy. Well, other than the dark shadows under Kriti's eyes. She still seemed to be keeping a low profile. DJ suspected she'd had time to think things over and was seeing Eliza in a new and not terribly flattering light.

"The general is totally hilarious with charades." DJ set the coffee pot back. "And it's fun." As in hint-hint, maybe Eliza should try it too.

"And helpful."

"Helpful?" DJ frowned. "What do you mean?"

"Nothing."

DJ decided to ignore whatever new game Eliza was playing. As she went back out to join the others, she saw that the snow had finally stopped. "Hey, it's clearing up out there," she pointed out.

"Yeah, but the lifts will be closing in about twenty minutes," said Conner.

"Not really enough time to go again," said Bradford.

So they started another round of charades — women against men — and the girls were just about to concede when Eliza waltzed in the front door with Harry. With her pink cheeks and perfect smile, it was difficult to believe that she'd been out partying last night. But perhaps she hadn't overdone it as badly as poor Kriti.

"We have a surprise for you," said Eliza as she came over to General Harding.

He grinned up at her. "What?"

"As a thank you for your wonderful hospitality, the girls and I have gotten you a little present." She tossed a quick warning look at DJ and Rhiannon, but they just watched with interest.

"It's a gift certificate for the River Trout Grille."

"Oh, that's a delightful restaurant," said the general. "The chef there is from New York and a real artist. How thoughtful of you."

"And we made a reservation for the two of you for this evening," gushed Eliza.

"Oh, my!" Grandmother clapped her hands. "That's wonderful, Eliza."

"Yes," said General Harding. "Delightful."

"Eight o'clock was the earliest we could get you in," said Eliza as she handed the certificate to the general. DJ peeked to see that it was for $200 — pretty generous, she thought. But then Eliza could afford it. And, really, it was kind of sweet. Maybe this was Eliza's way of apologizing for the stupidity that had transpired in the past couple of days.

General Harding looked at his watch. "Well, it takes about twenty minutes to get there, Katherine. I don't know about you, but I wouldn't mind a little nap first." He extended his hand to her.

"Definitely." She let him help her up.

"And you can go early for drinks and appetizers," suggested Eliza. "I asked them to hold you a small table in the lounge."

"You are a dear," said Grandmother as she patted Eliza on the cheek. "A lovely, lovely, dear."

"But I didn't get dinner catered tonight," said the general. "Being that they don't work on Sundays. I hope that's — "

"Not a problem," said Eliza. "We're big girls; we can fix our own dinner. Don't worry."

After the general and Grandmother were gone, DJ peered curiously at Eliza. "That was awfully nice of you. Do you want us to all reimburse you for the certificate?"

She waved her hand. "No, it's my treat."

"Well, thanks."

"See you later," she told them, giggling. Then she and Harry left.

"I wonder where they're going," mused DJ, not that she cared.

"Not to his place," said Bradford. "You can count on that."

"Well, you guys don't have to go back there either," said DJ. "Well, not until later that is. Feel free to hang out here as long as you like."

"You kids have a nice evening," said General Harding as he opened the front door for Grandmother.

"Bye-bye," called Eliza. "Y'all have a good time now!"

"We should be back around ten," called Grandmother.

Eliza stood by the window, watching. "There they go," she said in a cheerful voice.

"I can't believe he doesn't mind driving that huge thing around," said DJ as she observed the motor home pulling out of the circular driveway.

"It's probably very safe," said Rhiannon. "What time is it?"

DJ peeked at the big clock in the foyer. "A little before seven. The guys should be back soon."

"Yum ... pizza ..." Rhiannon smacked her lips. "What a great idea."

Eliza then pulled out her cell phone and soon was talking to someone on the other end. "Coast is clear," she said. "All systems go." Then she hung up.

"Who were you talking to?" asked DJ.

"Oh, you'll find out."

Now DJ was suspicious. "No, seriously," she said, "What's up?"

"Just a fun little surprise. That's all."

"What kind of surprise?" asked Rhiannon.

"Wait and see!" Then Eliza ran on up the stairs, giggling as she went.

It didn't take long to see what she was up to. Or to realize that Taylor and Casey were equally involved. First Garrison and Seth arrived with food. Lots of food. And Taylor and Casey began setting it out on the dining room table. Then, shortly after that, Harry arrived with a large box of bottles and began to set them up on top of the general's bar, which was securely locked.

"What are you doing?" demanded DJ when she realized what was going on.

"Getting ready for a nice little party."

"A nice little party?" She frowned at the bottles of hard liquor that he was lining up. "I don't think so."

"Now, don't worry," he assured her. "Eliza and I plan to do this with class. Not like the other night when my place got trashed."

"Class?" DJ stared at him. "How is that even possible?"

He chuckled. "You'll see."

"This is totally unacceptable!" she said loudly.

But that just made him laugh louder.

DJ was furious now. She glanced around, looking for Rhiannon for backup, but she wasn't around. DJ ran up the stairs.

"Rhiannon!" DJ yelled, going into the bedroom and startling poor Kriti who seemed to be taking refuge in their room.

"What's wrong?" asked Kriti in a quiet voice.

"Pizza here?" Rhiannon stuck her head out of the bathroom.

"No, the pizza is NOT here. And what's wrong is that Eliza and Harry are throwing a party."

Rhiannon frowned. "A party?"

"Right now, Harry is down there setting up a bar."

"Oh ..." Kriti looked concerned.

"I told him it was unacceptable, but he just laughed."

"What do we do?"

"I don't know." DJ slumped down onto a chair.

"Should we call your grandmother at the restaurant?"

DJ considered this. "I don't know ..."

"Maybe it won't be so bad," said Kriti.

"I can't believe you're supporting it," said DJ. "You were so wasted that you were throwing up—"

"As my father says, we learn by our mistakes," said Kriti. "If we are to grow, we must learn."

"But this is—"

"Lighten up, DJ." Taylor was now in the room. "Harry said you were flipping out down there. Can't you see that it's no big deal? Just a little get-together with our friends before we all go back to civilization tomorrow. Can't you just chill for once?"

"Chill?" DJ glared at Taylor. "This is not our house. The general has trusted us. My grandmother has trusted us. Eliza obviously set this up to get them out of the house so that—"

"But they're only going for dinner," said Taylor coolly. "They should be back, what? Around nine or—"

"Ten!"

"Okay, ten. But, seriously, what can happen between now and ten?"

DJ considered this. "I don't know."

"Well, I do know," said Taylor. "Just a few laughs, some food, and a few drinks. No one is going to get crazy tonight. Understand?"

DJ sighed. "No."

Rhiannon put a hand on her shoulder. "Taylor's probably right."

"There's not much you can do anyway," said Kriti. "Except govern yourself."

"Govern myself?" DJ frowned at Kriti.

"It's all anyone can do," Kriti continued as if she were an expert in this. "We only control our own actions."

"So are you drinking tonight?" DJ asked her.

Kriti solemnly shook her head. "No. Not even a sip."

Well, that was somewhat reassuring. Still, DJ did not like this. Not one little bit!

18

viva vermont!

"WHAT'S GOING ON HERE?" asked Conner when he came in the back door bearing pizza.

"You guys having a party?" asked Bradford.

DJ ushered them to the kitchen where Rhiannon was already waiting, and together the two girls explained.

"We didn't know what to do," said DJ. "I mean, I told both Harry and Eliza that this was totally unacceptable, but they just laughed."

"Big surprise there," said Bradford.

"We considered calling Mrs. Carter," said Rhiannon.

"But we felt bad about spoiling their evening." DJ shook her head. "They were such fun this afternoon. And, really, they've been good sports. They probably deserve a night out."

"Besides, as Taylor pointed out, the party has to end before ten since our chaperones will be getting home by then."

"That's true," said Conner. "I can't imagine Eliza wanting to risk getting caught."

"Exactly," said Rhiannon. "So, we're holing up in here."

"Running down the clock," added DJ as she peeked into the pizza box. "Looks good."

The four of them sat at the kitchen table eating pizza and trying to pretend there wasn't a party going on out there.

"Hey, what is this?" asked Seth as he came into the kitchen with an empty ice bucket. "Private party?"

"Yeah," said DJ grumpily, "and we'd like to keep it that way."

"Don't mind me," he said as he helped himself to the ice bin in the freezer.

"Two more hours," said DJ sadly.

"Maybe we should go out there and mix," suggested Conner. "Just to make sure nothing gets out of hand."

"Or broken," added Rhiannon with a concerned frown.

So the four of them crashed the party that they wished wasn't happening. To DJ's surprise, it wasn't just the guys from Harry's cabin. No, that would've been "too boring," according to Garrison, who explained, "We needed more chicks ... so these dudes would lay off our women." He had an arm draped around Casey's shoulder as if to show ownership.

DJ stared at Casey with narrowed eyes. Casey had a glass of something amber in her hand, but she avoided DJ's gaze. Well, why shouldn't she feel guilty? They should all feel guilty.

"This party ends at nine thirty," DJ said loudly.

But Garrison just laughed.

DJ went over to Rhiannon. "Man, would I love to knock some heads together."

"Love your neighbor ..." Rhiannon smiled. "But I do understand."

"This started out to be such a cool day," said DJ sadly.

"I know ..."

"I was thinking about what Kriti said. I mean, she's sort of right. We can't control these idiots, but does that mean we just stand by and watch?"

"I don't know . . ." Rhiannon shook her head.

"It's so frustrating."

"It's hard to know what's best. I guess we should just be glad that this can only go on for another—" She glanced at the clock. "Just over an hour."

"An hour of torture."

Just then they heard a crash in the dining room. "Oh no," said Rhiannon with wide eyes.

"I hope it wasn't anything expensive," said DJ as they hurried to see.

"Or irreplaceable."

Fortunately, it was only a glass pitcher, and Eliza seemed unconcerned.

"It's a crystal glass pitcher," Rhiannon pointed out.

"Put it on my bill," said Eliza. Then she nodded to Kriti and to the broken glass. "Can you get that, sweetie?"

DJ gave Kriti a look as if to say, "See what this gets you?" But Kriti seemed oblivious as she began to pick up the largest broken fragments and set them on a paper napkin.

"I need to get out of here," DJ told Conner. "If I stick around I might hurt someone."

"I'm with you," said Bradford. He'd just joined them.

"Let's go to the main lodge and see if we can get some cocoa or something," said Conner.

The music seemed to be louder now, and the house was crowded with people that DJ had never seen. Suddenly, she wasn't so sure they should just leave.

"It kills me to see this artwork at such risk," said Rhiannon.

"Should we take it down or anything?" asked DJ.

"Maybe the breakables," said Conner.

So the four of them gathered the items that seemed most at risk and carried them back to the laundry room, which seemed a fairly safe spot.

"Now let's take a break," said Conner.

Other than the bar, the lodge was pretty much closed. They all got cocoa out of a machine, sitting at one of the tables outside the cafeteria, waiting.

"This totally sucks." DJ set her cocoa down so hard that it splashed.

"I hear ya," agreed Conner.

"Well, it's almost nine thirty," said Bradford.

"Maybe it's time we go and remind them that the party's over," said Rhiannon.

They were all relieved to go back. DJ was hoping that by the time they got there, the cars would be heading out and Eliza and the others would be putting the general's lodge back together.

"I think there are even more cars," said DJ as they hurried to the back door.

"The music's even louder than before," said Rhiannon loudly as they went in the back way.

Even the kitchen had partiers in it now.

"Get out of here," demanded DJ. "The party's over!"

A guy who looked a lot older than high school peered curiously at her. "Is this your house?"

She considered this. "No, but it's my friend's house and—"

"Your friend is my friend." He held up his beer like he was toasting.

"Eliza!" yelled DJ as she stormed out of the kitchen, pushing her way past strangers. "Party's over!" she yelled again and again.

"What are you doing?" demanded Taylor. She and Eliza were standing in front of DJ now, looking at her as if she was the one with bad judgment.

"It's a quarter to ten," DJ said loudly. "The party's over!"

"That's right," said Rhiannon from behind her.

"Yeah," said Conner. "You guys don't have much time to clear this place out, Eliza."

"And to clean it up," added Bradford.

Taylor looked at Eliza, and they both started to laugh.

"You guys are losing it," said DJ as she grabbed Taylor by the arm. "The general and my grandmother will be back soon."

"I don't think so . . .." Eliza winked at Taylor. "Do you want to tell them, or should I?"

DJ got the worst feeling then. Seriously, she would put absolutely nothing past these two now. "What have you done to the general and my grandmother?"

"We've done nothing but given them a nice quiet evening away from the kiddies," said Eliza.

"They'll be perfectly comfortable in their little home on wheels," said Taylor.

"What are you saying?" demanded Rhiannon.

"Don't worry," said Eliza. "I just spoke to the general."

"What's going on?" asked DJ.

"They had a perfectly lovely dinner," said Taylor.

"And when they started to go home, they realized they had a little mechanical problem." Eliza gave DJ a sly grin.

"With no mechanics around on a Sunday night and holiday weekend." Taylor held up her hands in a helpless gesture.

"What?" DJ was suspicious now. "They *just happened* to break down?"

"Well . . . that's one way to look at it," said Eliza.

"Did you guys send someone up there to sabotage them?" DJ glared at Taylor.

"What on earth would make you jump to that conclusion?" Taylor put on her most innocent face.

"Anyway," continued Eliza lightly, "when the general called here to check on us, I told him not to worry, that we were just fine and would probably just call it an early evening."

"They'll camp out in the general's motor home," said Taylor.

"Naturally, the general offered your grandmother the bedroom, and he'll use the pull-out bed in the couch."

"End of story," said Taylor.

DJ honestly felt lightheaded now, like she was about to faint.

"Come on," said Rhiannon to DJ. "Let's go upstairs and regroup."

With Conner and Rhiannon guiding her, they went upstairs, but when they opened the door to the room the four girls were sharing, they saw that it had been invaded.

"Get out of here!" screamed DJ. Then she actually picked up a chair and acted like she was about to throw it at the surprised couple.

"Easy does it," said Conner as he gently removed the chair from her hands.

"But she's right," yelled Bradford, "Get out of here!"

The couple grabbed up a couple of items of clothing and ran for the door. DJ collapsed into a chair and held her head in her hands. "What a mess."

"Maybe Conner and I should head up there and help the general with his mechanical problem," suggested Bradford.

"For all we know they might be enjoying themselves," said DJ.

"It's a very nice motor home," said Rhiannon, "With all the comforts of home. They should be perfectly comfortable."

"Still ..." DJ stood now. "Maybe I should just call the police."

They all paused to consider this.

"I'd just tell them the truth," she said eagerly. "That someone had thrown a party here, without permission, and that there was underage drinking."

"Of course, that would mean that the general and your grandmother would hear about it."

"I know." DJ nodded. "Right now I don't even care."

"And Eliza, Taylor, and Casey will be in serious hot water," added Rhiannon. "Not that I particularly care."

"And the guys too," pointed out Conner.

"I don't know." Bradford frowned. "It seems wrong to rat on your friends."

"How about if we warn them first?" suggested DJ.

"Yeah," said Rhiannon.

So it was decided they would warn the party hosts. "But we'll stick to our guns, right?" said DJ as they trooped back down the stairs.

"Absolutely," said Conner.

"We'll tell them they have twenty minutes," said DJ.

"To get everyone out of here," added Rhiannon.

"And all the alcohol too."

At the foot of the stairs, they gathered to put the finishing touches on their end-the-party plan. And then, sharing high fives all the way around, the Fearsome Foursome went to work.

19

viva vermont!

RHIANNON HEADED FOR THE CD PLAYER, which was cranked up so high that DJ thought she could feel the wood floor shaking, or maybe that was the dancers. DJ, backed by Conner and Bradford, and all armed with cell phones, confronted Eliza and Harry in the middle of the dance floor.

DJ nodded to Rhiannon and suddenly the music stopped.

"The party is over!" DJ shouted.

"That's right!" yelled Conner.

"You have ten minutes to clear this place out!" shouted Bradford.

"The police will be here shortly!" DJ looked out the front window for dramatic effect.

Fortunately, this last bit of news seemed to get the partiers' attention.

"And don't break anything on your way out!" warned Rhiannon.

"Security cameras are running!" added Bradford.

"And just in case, license plate numbers will be taken," added DJ.

Amazingly, almost the whole house was cleared out in less than two minutes.

"What do you guys think you're doing?" demanded Taylor.

"Calling the police," said DJ calmly.

"You've lost your freaking mind," said Seth.

"You guys are totally spoiling everything," said Eliza.

"No!" DJ stared at Taylor and Eliza now. "You guys are the ones spoiling everything! We are totally serious; we will be calling the police if every ounce of booze isn't out of here in three minutes."

"Or we can save you the trouble and pour it down the drain," said Conner as he picked up a bottle of vodka and headed for the kitchen.

Harry made a dash to the bar and began gathering his bottles and loading them back into the cardboard box. "The party's moving to my place," he called as he headed for the door. "Let's get away from these losers."

"We'll be there in a minute," called Eliza as she ran to get her parka.

"You're not going anywhere until this place is cleaned up," called DJ.

"That's right," said Bradford, stopping Taylor in her tracks.

"Otherwise, you're *going down*." DJ couldn't help but chuckle at this line, and suddenly the Fearsome Foursome were all laughing.

"Don't think we don't mean it," said Rhiannon, stifling laughter.

"I think you guys have totally lost it." Eliza rolled her eyes.

"I think they've just saved you from getting into serious trouble," said Kriti in a quiet voice. She'd been on the sidelines watching it all unfold.

"Just to show we're good sports, we'll help you clean up," said Rhiannon. "So let's get moving."

"Oh, I don't know," said Bradford reluctantly. "I might not be *that* good of a sport."

"Come on," urged DJ. "There's a lot of work to be done."

Casey had been pretty quiet through the whole confrontation, and DJ wasn't sure what she was thinking, but suddenly she seemed to switch sides. "Come on," Casey said to Taylor and Eliza. "We better get to work. This place really is a mess. We don't want the general and Mrs. Carter to come home to this."

Although Taylor and Eliza complained loudly, they did start to clean things up. Even Kriti helped out, and DJ thought she seemed relieved by this turn of events.

"So?" DJ stopped Kriti from sweeping the kitchen floor. "You still say we can only control ourselves?"

Kriti leaned on the broom to consider this. "Sometimes . . . I think it takes a community to bring about change."

"Or a village to raise an idiot?"

Kriti smiled. "Yes. Something like that."

"Wow, this place was *really* a mess," said Casey as she hauled another full garbage bag through the kitchen and toward the back door. Conner was letting them put the trash in his pickup for now. He would find a place to dump it tomorrow.

"Can you imagine how it would've looked if the party had kept on going?" asked DJ as she wiped down a granite countertop.

Eliza closed the door of the full dishwasher, just one of several loads since the partiers had helped themselves to the general's glassware. "I have to admit that it did get out of hand," she said as she turned on the appliance.

"Ya think?" DJ stared at Eliza in disbelief.

"Yes ... I suppose we should thank you for putting an end to it."

"She didn't *end* anything," said Taylor. "The party is still going strong at Harry's place."

"You mean the pigsty," said Conner with disgust.

"Pigsty or not, I'm heading over there right now." Taylor pulled on her parka. "You coming, Eliza?"

"Not tonight," said Eliza. "I've got a headache."

"Aw, too bad for you." Taylor zipped her jacket and looked around the kitchen. "Looks like you guys have the cleaning under control here. I'm sure you won't miss me."

"If you go over to Harry's tonight, you better not expect to find the back door unlocked when you come back," threatened DJ.

"Yeah, whatever." Taylor looked over at Casey now. "You coming, Casey?"

"I ... uh ..." Casey bit her lower lip.

"I mean what I said, Casey." DJ put as much authority as she could muster into her voice. "That key will NOT be under the bear tonight."

"Come on, Casey," urged Taylor. "Don't be stuck here cleaning house with a bunch of loser party poopers. Let's go have some fun, girlfriend."

"I think I'll pass," said Casey. "I'm actually kind of tired anyway."

Taylor scowled at her. "Yeah, right."

DJ locked eyes with Taylor. "That door will be locked, Taylor. No key. Understood?" Taylor just shrugged. "Like I care." Then she grinned. "Night-night, party poopers."

The house was pretty much back to order by one in the morning. By that time, Eliza seemed genuinely sorry.

"You know, I'm sorry about everything," she told DJ as they headed upstairs. The guys were gone now, and all the doors securely locked. "I just didn't think the party would get out of hand like that. Harry was surprised too. He hadn't expected crashers . . . but then what do you do?"

DJ paused to look into Eliza's face. "Can you imagine what this place might've looked like in the morning if it had gone on like that? Or what the general would've said when he saw his house totally trashed? Or how your parents would've felt if the cops had come out and you'd been arrested?"

"Yeah, it really was a stupid idea. I can't believe I let Taylor talk me into it."

DJ felt a strange sliver of relief. "So, it really was Taylor's idea?"

"Oh, yeah. She planned the whole thing. I'll admit it sounded pretty good at first—a Viva Vermont party to celebrate our last night up here. And, naturally, Harry loved the idea."

"Yeah, especially since he wasn't the real host. If things got broken or the place got busted—what difference would it make to Harry? He could duck out the back door, but you and Taylor and Casey would be the ones called on the carpet, Eliza. You'd be held responsible."

"Guess I didn't really think of that."

They paused in the hallway between the bedrooms, and Eliza put a hand on DJ's shoulder. "You know Taylor can be really convincing. I should know better than to get pulled into her schemes, but she has this way—you know—when she turns on the charm, and it starts to sound so good."

"I know."

"But sometimes she scares me too."

DJ nodded. "Yeah, she scares me too—but mostly for her own welfare. Sometimes I think she's going to totally self-destruct."

"I guess there's not much we can do about that." Then Eliza said goodnight and went into her room.

But DJ just stood there in the darkened hallway. Okay, as angry as she felt toward Taylor, she was worried too. Taylor was a mess. And she deserved to get into trouble. But what if that foolish girl came back here wasted in the wee hours of the morning and couldn't get into the house? It was probably about twenty degrees out there at night.

DJ trudged back down the stairs again. She unlocked the back door, tucked the key under the bear, locked the door again, and then went to bed exhausted.

When DJ woke up the next morning, Taylor was sleeping snugly in her bunk. Well, it figured. Still, it was better than finding the girl's frozen body on the back porch. Hopefully, now that DJ had stood up to her the way she had last night, it would be easier to stand up to her again—and perhaps even go to her grandmother if Taylor didn't straighten up.

All the girls except Taylor, who was probably hung over, got in a lot of good rides on Monday. The snow was perfect, the sky was blue, and everyone was in good spirits. The general and Grandmother made it back home just before noon—also in good spirits. By three o'clock, they had loaded up the motor home and were ready to roll.

"Did you girls have a good time?" asked the general as he started the big diesel engine.

They all chimed in saying that it had been great, thanking him for inviting them up and chauffeuring them around in his fancy rig. Naturally, no mention had been made of last night's near fiasco. Not that DJ had decided yet whether or not to tell her grandmother.

"Maybe we can do this again," General Harding called out as he pulled onto the highway. "How about Thanksgiving, Katherine?"

DJ let out a low groan and didn't hear her grandmother's response. It was a generous offer, but right now the last thing she wanted to do was to come up here with the Carter House girls. Or at least some of them. Not unless things changed.

Taylor was already asleep on the big bed in the back, with Eliza and Casey on either side of her. Just like none of last night had ever happened. Meanwhile, Kriti, Rhiannon, and DJ played cards at the dining room table, watching the scenery pass by them.

"Really," said Rhiannon, "It wasn't that bad, was it, DJ?"

Suddenly, DJ remembered how they'd sung praise songs on the mountain on Sunday and smiled. "No, it was actually pretty great."

A few hours later, they were rolling into town. By this time, all six of the girls were packed into the general's bedroom, visiting and actually getting along again—for the first time in days.

"Hey, my phone is finally working," said Rhiannon. And so they were all checking their phones.

"Any more hate mail?" asked Casey as she closed her own phone.

DJ considered this. "Come to think of it, I haven't had a mean text message since Saturday. Do you think she gave up on me?"

"Maybe so."

DJ remembered the handshake at the swim meet and how she and Haley had actually exchanged some semi-friendly words.

"Maybe Haley has finally decided to move on," said Casey.

"Although I do have one missed call." DJ pushed her caller ID. "Oh, it's just Conner." She paused to listen.

"DJ!" he said in an urgent tone that almost didn't sound like him. "I just got back in town—it's about four o'clock now—I'm at the hospital—and I don't know how to tell you this, but it's Haley. She's, uh, she's in critical condition—she—she tried to kill herself. Call me when you get this. Or if it's not too late, come by the hospital. She's in the critical care unit. I really need you here."

"Oh no!" DJ shook her head and then actually replayed the message to be sure she'd heard it correctly.

"What's wrong?" asked Casey.

DJ felt like her head was spinning, like she needed to grab onto something and hold on tight before she fell sideways. "Oh no!" she cried.

"What is it?" said Rhiannon.

"What's going on, DJ?" demanded Eliza.

"It's—it's Haley—"

"Is she threatening you again?" asked Taylor.

DJ dumbly shook her head.

"What is it then?" demanded Casey.

"Yeah," said Taylor. "You've got us all in suspense now. Out with it!"

DJ swallowed hard, still trying to get her bearings. "It's Haley ... she's in the hospital ... critical condition ... she ... she tried to kill herself."

Instantly, they were all pressing her for details. "When? How? Where? Why?"

"I don't know." DJ just shook her head. "But I have a strong feeling that it's because of me. Conner told me to come to the hospital." And now tears began to flow. The idea of Haley—suicide—what if she hadn't made it? It was all too much.

The girls all gathered around her now, holding her as she cried, telling her it was going to be okay, that Haley was probably just fine. But DJ didn't think so. She'd heard the desperate tone of Conner's voice—like he was afraid. And when she tried his number, it went straight to voicemail. She knew that wasn't good. Deep inside of her, she knew that this was serious. Very serious. And she knew that it had a lot to do with her. Oh, what if Haley was dead?

20

viva vermont!

THE GENERAL DROPPED DJ OFF at the hospital. Even Grandmother seemed concerned. "You call and let us know how your friend is," she said.

As DJ rode the elevator up to CCU, she tried not to think about the fact that Haley did not consider DJ a friend—or that Haley probably hated DJ more than anyone on the planet. Or that DJ was probably the main reason behind this horrible tragedy.

In some ways, it seemed crazy to even show up here, but on the other hand, Conner had begged her to come. If nothing else, she could comfort him. Still, as she walked down the hall she felt unsure. What if Haley's family knew about DJ? What if Bethany or Amy were here? What would DJ say?

"I tried to call you," she told Conner when she located him in the waiting area outside of CCU. He got up quickly to meet her. She couldn't help but notice Bethany and Amy, both glaring at her, as well as an older couple who looked extremely sad. DJ knew they had to be Haley's parents. She avoided their eyes. "Is Haley—I mean, is she still ..."

"She's still in critical condition ... sleeping."

DJ shot up a silent thank-you prayer.

"Let's go over there to talk." Conner pointed to a couple of chairs down the hall. But even as they walked, DJ could feel them all looking at her, as if their eyes were burning holes in her back. Of course, they'd blame her. Why wouldn't they?

"This is all my fault, isn't it?" she said as they sat down.

"No … not really. I mean, yes, in a weird way, I suppose it seems that way. Haley has blamed you for everything that's gone wrong lately. Not that it makes sense. But you know about that."

"Has she spoken to you?" asked DJ.

"Just barely. Mostly she just sleeps."

"Do you think she'll be okay?"

Conner sighed and shook his head. "I don't know. The doctors can't really say yet."

"What happened? How did she do it? When?"

"Just last night. She overdosed on aspirin —"

"On aspirin?"

"That's right."

DJ considered this. "Aspirin? That doesn't sound too serious."

"That's what I thought too … at first anyway." Then he explained how a lot of people assume that aspirin is no big deal. "But the truth is it's highly toxic when you take a large dose. I overheard some nurses talking about it. It sounds like they see this occasionally—like a person can write a suicide note and take an overdose of aspirin for attention, without realizing how extremely lethal it really is."

"So they don't really want to die?" DJ was trying to grasp this.

"No, it's more like a way to get attention, you know, a really sad cry for help."

"Do you think that's what Haley did?"

"That's what her mom told me."

"Oh ... that is so sad."

"Yeah ..." Conner just shook his head. DJ could tell that he felt as responsible as she did.

"But she made it to the hospital," said DJ. "Isn't there a way to treat this—I mean, whatever it is?"

"They pumped her stomach late last night ... but the aspirin had already gotten into her system. It had begun to damage her kidneys and liver."

"Oh no ..."

"She may not recover. Haley's dad told me that aspirin poisoning can be a slow and painful death."

"Oh ..." Now DJ was crying again. "I just feel ... like ... like this is my fault."

"It's not your fault, DJ. I mean, not directly. You're involved, yes, just like I'm involved. But you need to realize that we didn't cause this. It was Haley's choice, not ours."

"I know her friends already hate me, but her parents must hate me too."

"No, it's not like that. I've talked to them, and they sort of understand what caused this. Oh, sure, they're in shock and they're grieving. But they were fully aware of Haley's OCD, and they knew she'd been acting differently lately."

"Apparently she's the one who's been texting me."

"I'm not surprised."

"Casey saw her at school."

"And there's more to tell you, DJ."

"More?"

"Yeah ... I'd rather you hear it from me."

"Okay ..."

"Well, remember Dirk? He's a friend of Garrison's. He was up at Ashton Peak and—"

"Oh, yeah, yeah—the short blond guy. I remember him."

"It seems that he and Amy had just started dating ... and he called her from up there, and they were just talking, you know, and he told Amy the hot rumor about you and me—"

"That we slept together?"

Conner nodded solemnly.

"But it's a lie, Conner. We both know that. Yeah, we shared a bed, but that was it. Why does everyone act like that?"

"We know it's a lie, DJ, but Amy believed Dirk. And, of course, she told Haley. Later that same night, well, Haley did this."

"I feel kind of sick," said DJ suddenly.

"I know—"

"No, I mean for real." She shot off toward a bathroom across the hall, went straight for a stall, and waited to throw up. Her hands and knees were shaking, and her head was hot, but she felt cold all over. Still, she didn't throw up. After a few minutes, she emerged from the stall, went to the sink, and splashed cold water on her face—just leaning over and splashing for a long time—wishing she could wash this whole thing away.

"Are you okay?" asked a woman's concerned voice.

DJ looked up to see Haley's mother—she was certain of it. The woman held out some paper towels. DJ nodded, thanked her, then dried her face.

"This is so sad," said DJ.

The woman nodded. "I'm Mrs. Callahan."

"I know." DJ threw the towels away. "I'm so, so sorry ... about Haley."

"Thank you."

Now DJ didn't know what more to say. Really, what did you say to the parent of a dying child?

"I saw you swim on Friday, DJ. You did very well." DJ frowned. "Yeah ... but I beat Haley."

"I watched you when you went to Haley ... how you shook her hand."

"Yeah, but ..."

"But Haley also thinks you stole her boyfriend."

DJ nodded.

"Conner has explained it all to me."

"Everything?"

"Yes. Even your unfortunate night in Everett Falls."

"We didn't do anything, honest. I'm a Christian. I don't do that—"

"Conner told us that too."

"I'm just so worried about Haley." DJ felt tears coming again. She grabbed a tissue to blot them. "I wish there was something I could do. I just feel so bad ..."

"Well, you said you're a Christian, DJ. Pray for her."

"I have been praying. Even before this whole thing happened. I'd been praying and hoping that we could be friends again."

"Just for the record, Haley actually admires you a lot."

"She admires me?"

"Well, she probably hates you too, but I'm sure you know that."

DJ felt slightly confused now. What was this woman really saying?

"It's just that she'd talked about you to me, DJ. From what she'd told me, I had assumed you were good friends. But then Haley is a master at hiding her feelings. She's learned to cover her obsessions. I knew she'd been acting oddly. I suppose I should've put two and two together when she was praising a girl who was both her competition in the pool as well as with her ex-boyfriend."

"But Conner and I are *just* friends. We've tried to tell everyone—"

"That's not really the point, DJ. For Haley it's all about perception. Sometimes she sees things differently than the rest of us. She takes things harder, puts more pressure on herself."

"Conner told me about that."

"But I thought she was fine. She seemed to have made a good adjustment to moving back to town; she seemed happy to be back on swim team and making new friends. I suppose I sort of let my guard down." Now Mrs. Callahan was starting to cry.

DJ grabbed a tissue and handed it to her. "But you can't blame yourself."

She blotted her eyes and nodded, and DJ just stood there without the vaguest idea of what to do. This was all so sad ... painfully sad. Why had Haley done this?

"I hope I didn't say too much, DJ."

"No, not at all."

"I better go check on Haley now."

DJ nodded. "I really meant it. I'll keep praying for her."

"Maybe ... if she feels up to it ... maybe you could talk to her. I actually think that would help her get better."

DJ frowned. She wasn't so sure. Still, maybe Haley's mom knew best. "Okay ... if you really think it's a good idea."

Mrs. Callahan nodded, blew her nose, and left. DJ took in a deep breath and slowly exhaled. Feeling slightly more steady, she went out to find Conner.

"Everything okay in there?" he asked with concern.

"Haley's mom is really nice."

"I know."

"Let's call everyone we know to pray for Haley."

"I've already called the church."

"And I told the girls."

"Maybe we should go and pray too."

So they went to the chapel, and, kneeling down up at the front, they both bowed their heads and silently prayed.

Two days passed without much of a change in Haley's condition. During this time she mostly slept, although Conner said he'd had a short conversation with her on Tuesday night. But, like she'd promised Mrs. Callahan, DJ stopped by the hospital to check on Haley, and she continued to pray for her. Even if Haley didn't respond, DJ had decided to stick it out. Sometimes she'd have to lurk in the hallway, waiting for Bethany or Amy or Haley's parents to end their visits. Then DJ would just stand by Haley's bed and simply talk to her. She told her how sorry she was for how things had gone and how she wanted Haley to get better and how she was praying and how she hoped they could be friends again. Sometimes it felt crazy and weird and generally hopeless, but DJ didn't want to give up.

By Friday, it started to look better for Haley. The prognosis had gotten more hopeful, and some of Haley's lab tests were improving. More importantly, Haley had been awake for most of the day. Her mother left DJ a voicemail message asking her to stop by to see Haley. Suddenly, DJ wasn't so sure. It was one thing to talk to an unconscious Haley—what would she say to her if she was awake?

Haley's skin looked a little less sallow. Her eyes, although they still had dark shadows beneath them, seemed a bit less sunken ... though they looked somewhat lifeless. For a moment, DJ almost turned back. But when Haley saw DJ approaching, she almost seemed to brighten.

"Hey, DJ ..." Haley spoke softly.

"Hey ..." DJ smiled and moved closer to Haley's bed. By now she was fairly used to all the tubes and machines connected to Haley. "How's it going?"

"Better, I guess ..." Haley gave her sad little smile.

DJ wasn't sure what to say. "I've been by to see you, but you were always sleeping."

"That's what Mom said."

"But I've been praying for you a lot."

"Thanks."

"I mean, I prayed for you before all this happened too. I guess I've been worried about you for a while, Haley."

"I'm surprised you don't hate me."

"No." DJ shook her head. "Of course not."

"But you know I was the one sending you those stupid hate messages?"

DJ waved her hand. "Hey, that's all over with now."

"I'm sorry."

"I'm sorry too." DJ took in a long breath. "And I'm not sure that it matters, but Conner and I really are just friends. That thing about us having sex is totally bogus. I mean, if you were worried ..."

"I know. Conner told me about it."

"If I'd known ... well, you know ... that it was going to go like this ... well, I wouldn't have even gotten involved with him again. Even just as friends. I mean, it really did seem too soon. I knew you were hurting and ..."

"Look, DJ, it's my fault that I'm here." Haley's voice sounded a little stronger now, like she actually believed this. "I realize that I have to take responsibility for that."

"Yeah ..."

"And the truth is this whole thing is pretty humiliating."

"Huh?"

"I mean, it seemed like a great idea at first … but it's not like I really thought it out too well. Look at everything I've put everyone, including myself, through. Pretty pathetic … and embarrassing."

"I guess I get that."

"The thing is I didn't really, truly want to die, not even when I did it. I mean, I did feel kind of hopeless and everything. Somehow, chugging down a bottle of aspirin, well, it seemed like an answer at the time."

"Oh …"

"I sort of thought that it was just aspirin, like you know — no big deal."

"But it is a big deal. A huge deal. I mean, you could be dead."

"I realize that now. Anyway, at one point, after I'd been in the hospital a couple of days and I was feeling really, really sick, I actually did want to die. Just to get it over with — for everyone's sake."

DJ frowned and put her hand on Haley's arm. "But do you still feel like that?"

"No. I want to live now."

"Oh … good." DJ smiled. "I want you to live too."

"I obviously still have a lot of stuff to figure out … and things I need to deal with. But I'm not ready to give up."

"Yeah … life is hard … I actually know that from experience. I mean, stuff happens … stuff we can't control." Suddenly, DJ began telling Haley about her mom's death and her dad's rejection. It wasn't anything she'd planned to share, but somehow it all just spilled out.

"I had no idea." Haley sighed. "I thought you had this perfectly wonderful life. I mean, hey, you're a Carter House girl."

DJ actually laughed now. "Well, take it from me, that is highly overrated."

"So ... when I get out of here, DJ, well, I hope we can be friends."

"Absolutely!"

They talked awhile longer, but DJ could see that Haley was getting sleepy. "I'll see you tomorrow," she promised her.

"Yeah, see ya."

As DJ walked through the waiting area, she noticed Bethany and Amy coming her way. She started to smile and wave to them, but they just narrowed their eyes, stepping aside to let her pass and then hurrying from her as if she might contaminate them. As they went by DJ, she heard Bethany whisper, "Poison."

Sure, it hurt. But DJ decided to shrug it off. Really, what did silly Bethany know? DJ felt genuinely hopeful about how it had gone with Haley just now. Why let anyone spoil that? As Grandmother liked to say, "Rome wasn't built in a day." DJ knew that repairing every single broken relationship wasn't going to happen in one day either. Still, she felt that with God anything was possible. Really, what couldn't God do? Shooting up a silent prayer, she turned around and followed Bethany and Amy back to the waiting area.

LOST IN LAS VEGAS

carter house girls

MELODY CARLSON

bestselling author

Read chapter 1 of *Lost in Las Vegas*, Book 5 in Carter House Girls.

LOST in Las Vegas

"Remind me to never, ever star in another high school musical again." Eliza sighed dramatically as she poured her coffee. It was the Sunday morning after the final performance of *South Pacific* and DJ suspected that Eliza was just fishing for compliments. Not that she hadn't already gotten plenty. And last night, she'd been presented with a huge bouquet of roses. DJ knew they were from Eliza's parents, but Eliza received them like an Oscar.

"But what if Mr. Harper really does *High School Musical* in the spring?" asked Kriti with wide, dark eyes. DJ could tell by the way Kriti said this that she was hoping he would. Eliza probably was too.

"That is so last week," said Taylor.

"Meaning you wouldn't participate in it?" Eliza pushed a long strand of blonde hair over her shoulder and sat up straighter, looking directly at Taylor like this was a personal challenge.

Taylor rolled her eyes, then reached for the fruit platter. "Meaning I don't really want to think about it right now. Sheesh, Eliza, didn't you just ask us to remind you *never* to be in another musical?"

"Eliza is probably just trying to secure her next starring role," said Rhiannon. Then she frowned like she hadn't really meant it to sound like that. "And why shouldn't she?" she added quickly. "Eliza was absolutely fantastic as Nurse Nellie. Everyone said so."

"And it's obvious that Eliza never wants us to forget that she was a star," teased Casey.

"*Was.*" Taylor chuckled. "As in she's a has-been now."

Some of the girls snickered, but Eliza just glared at Taylor.

Then as if she'd just started listening, Grandmother cleared her throat and closed the open date book that she'd been studying. She looked at the girls. "I see there are only two weeks remaining until winter break, ladies." She shook her head sadly. "I just can't believe that it's already December. It seems like only yesterday that you girls arrived at Carter House. My, my, how time flies."

"And the Winter Ball is next Saturday," Eliza reminded them. As if anyone could've forgotten with all the posters plastered all over the school. But DJ was still unsure. Conner had asked her to go, but she hadn't agreed. Even though Haley hadn't returned to school yet, it still made DJ uncomfortable to be seen as more than "just friends" with Conner. And DJ knew that Haley's swim-team buddies were probably reporting to her.

"My mother and I are shopping for gowns today," continued Eliza. She glanced at her roommate. "And Kriti too, of course."

I already have my dress," said Taylor. "A little something my mother sent over from Milan while she was performing there last month."

DJ could tell this little dig was aimed directly at Eliza. The two girls had been going at it steadily for the last couple of weeks. It had started when Eliza's boyfriend, Harry, had made what Eliza interpreted as a flirtatious move toward Taylor during a rehearsal for the musical. Actually, DJ had seen it herself and, although she hadn't told anyone, she felt certain that Harry had been flirting too. But he'd been unaware that Eliza had been watching at the time. Yet, in a way, DJ was glad Eliza and Taylor were at odds again. They had all experienced those two "power forces" united during last month's ski trip—and it had been a rather frightening experience. Sort of like it might be if Russia and China ever got together.

"My mother offered to shop for a gown for me in Paris," said Eliza, her attempt at one-upping Taylor. "But I told her to wait. I wouldn't want to risk having a dress that fit poorly."

"That's why God invented alterations, Eliza," said Taylor. "Or perhaps you don't have such conveniences down south."

"I don't see why girls think they need to go out and spend a bunch of money on something new for a silly dance," said Casey. She glanced at Rhiannon, and DJ suspected that Casey was trying to make her feel better. "I mean you'll wear that dress like one time. What a waste!"

"So what do you intend to wear?" asked Eliza with a bored sort of interest. "Your Doc Martins and something with spikes?"

Casey made a face. "Actually, I might go eighties retro. Like Madonna or Blondie."

"Right." Eliza turned up her nose. "The Winter Ball theme is 'White Christmas' and we're supposed to dress in a fifties style of Hollywood elegance."

"You take those posters literally?" asked Casey.

"They suggested dresses in Christmas colors of red, green, or white." Eliza continued like she was reading it from a brochure.

"I think it'll be pretty," said Kriti.

"I intend to look for something sparkly in white to show off my tan," said Eliza.

"Fake tan." Taylor pushed a curly dark strand of hair away from her face and laughed. "My dress is black."

"It figures." Eliza snickered.

"I'm going to wear green," said Rhiannon quickly, like she was trying to keep this from escalating.

"What do you mean 'it figures'?" demanded Taylor.

"Everyone else will look Christmassy in red, green, or white, and the vamp will show up wearing black." Eliza laughed.

"Speaking of Winter Break," said Grandmother loudly. "What exactly are your plans, ladies?" She opened her date book and picked up her silver pen. "I'd like to make note of it now, if you don't mind."

"I'll be in France for Christmas," Eliza announced proudly.

"So you'll be flying directly to France from Connecticut?" inquired Grandmother.

"Actually, I'll spend the first week or so in Kentucky," admitted Eliza. "Visiting with friends and family. Then my older siblings and I will travel together just before Christmas. My mother said the rooms aren't completely renovated yet. Her designer, a well-known Parisian, promises to have it completed before Christmas Eve."

"La-di-da," said Casey.

Grandmother frowned at Casey. "So, how about you, Miss Atwood? When will you be departing for California?"

"The same day that school is out."

Grandmother made note of this.

"And I'll be leaving the day after school is out," said Rhiannon.

Grandmother's brows lifted with curiosity. "To go where, dear?"

"To an aunt who lives in Maine."

Grandmother smiled. "That's nice. I didn't know you had an aunt, Rhiannon."

"I didn't either. She's actually a great aunt and ..." Rhiannon paused as if unsure. "My mother may be joining me up there."

"Really?" Grandmother looked a bit skeptical, and everyone else got quiet. They all knew that Rhiannon's mother was in drug rehab—the lockdown kind.

"Yes. If my aunt signs something, they'll release her for the holidays."

"Very interesting." Grandmother looked at Kriti now. "I assume you'll be in New York?"

Kriti nodded happily. "Yes. We have some relatives coming from India to visit. My mother is very excited."

"Well, I'm sure you'll have a delightful Christmas." Grandmother frowned with realization. "I suppose you don't call it Christmas, do you, Kriti?"

Kriti looked slightly embarrassed. "It's a different sort of holiday, Mrs. Carter. We celebrate things like love, affection, sharing, and the renewing of family bonds."

"That sounds lovely." Grandmother looked at Taylor now. "And what will you be doing during the holidays, dear?"

Taylor sighed. "My mother has invited me to tour with her."

Grandmother's eyes lit up. She was a huge fan of Eva Perez. "Where will she be touring? Europe still?"

"I wish. No, she'll be in the southwest by then. And it looks like we'll be spending Christmas in Las Vegas."

Eliza snickered. "Charming."

Taylor tossed her a warning glance. "Hey, Las Vegas has its perks."

"Most importantly is that you're with family, Taylor." Grandmother smiled. "Isn't that what Christmas is all about?"

Taylor shrugged. "I guess."

Now Grandmother looked at DJ. "Now, you're still certain you don't want to join your father and his family for Christmas, Desiree?"

"No, Grandmother." DJ tried not to show frustration. But she and Grandmother had already been over this. The last place DJ wanted to be during Christmas break was with her father's happy little family. It was bad enough that this would be her first Christmas without her mother. But to be stuck playing the live-in babysitter to the toddler twins was unimaginable.

"Well, I'm sure that we'll have a delightful time right here at home." Grandmother smiled at DJ. "Perhaps we'll have the general over."

DJ got sympathetic glances from Rhiannon and Casey, and maybe even Kriti. Not that she wanted their pity. But Eliza just smiled smugly. And Taylor, well, she was a hard one to read.

But later that day, after DJ and Rhiannon got back from church, Taylor asked DJ if she was happy about her "holiday plans."

DJ groaned as she flopped onto her bed. "Holiday plans? Like I planned any of this?"

Taylor laughed. "Yeah, I guess not."

"I'll be fine," DJ assured her. "I'll catch up on sleep and reading."

"Maybe Conner will be around to keep you entertained," Taylor said in a sexy-sounding, teasing tone.

"Conner is going with his family to Montana for two weeks."

"Bummer."

"Tell me about it."

"I know!" Taylor exclaimed. "You'll come out to Las Vegas and visit me for Christmas."

DJ just laughed. "Oh, yeah, like that's going to happen."

"Why not?" Taylor looked slightly hurt.

"Seriously, Christmas in Las Vegas?"

"Why not?"

"Well, besides the fact that it sounds totally crazy, I know that my grandmother would never—in a million years—agree to something like that." And the truth was that DJ was secretly relieved for this excuse. Because, really, the only thing she could imagine being worse than spending Christmas with Grandmother in Connecticut or her father's family in California, would be to spend Christmas in Las Vegas with Taylor Mitchell.

Carter House Girls Series
from Melody Carlson

Mix six teenage girls and one '60s fashion icon (retired, of course) in an old Victorian-era boarding home. Add boys and dating, a little high school angst, and throw in a Kate Spade bag or two ... and you've got the Carter House Girls, Melody Carlson's new chick lit series for young adults!

Mixed Bags
Book One
Softcover • ISBN: 978-0-310-71488-0

Stealing Bradford
Book Two
Softcover • ISBN: 978-0-310-71489-7

Homecoming Queen
Book Three
Softcover • ISBN: 978-0-310-71490-3

Books 5–8 coming soon!

Pick up a copy today at your favorite bookstore!

Visit www.zondervan.com/teen

Forbidden Doors

A Four-Volume Series from Bestselling Author Bill Myers!

Some doors are better left unopened.

Join teenager Rebecca "Becka" Williams, her brother Scott, and her friend Ryan Riordan as they head for mind-bending clashes between the forces of darkness and the kingdom of God.

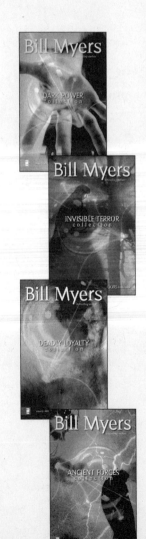

Dark Power Collection
Volume One

Softcover • ISBN: 978-0-310-71534-4

Contains books 1-3: *The Society,*
The Deceived, and *The Spell*

Invisible Terror Collection
Volume Two

Softcover • ISBN: 978-0-310-71535-1

Contains books 4-6: *The Haunting,*
The Guardian, and *The Encounter*

Deadly Loyalty Collection
Volume Three

Softcover • ISBN: 978-0-310-71536-8

Contains books 7-9: *The Curse,*
The Undead, and *The Scream*

Ancient Forces Collection
Volume Four

Softcover • ISBN: 978-0-310-71537-5

Contains books 10-12: *The Ancients,*
The Wiccan, and *The Cards*

The Shadowside Trilogy
by Robert Elmer!

Those who live in lush comfort on the bright side of the small planet Corista have plundered the water resources of Shadowside for centuries, ignoring the existence of Shadowside's inhabitants, who are nothing more than animals. Or so the Brightsiders have been taught. It will take a special young woman to expose the truth—and to help avert the war that is sure to follow—in the exciting Shadowside Trilogy, the latest sci-fi adventure from Robert Elmer.

Trion Rising
Book One
Softcover • ISBN: 978-0-310-71421-7

When the mysterious Jesmet, whom the authorities brand as a Magician of the Old Order, begins to connect with Oriannon, he is banished forever to the shadow side of their planet Corista.

The Owling
Book Two
Softcover • ISBN: 978-0-310-71422-4

Life is turned upside down on Corista for 15-year-old Oriannon and her friends. The planet's axis has shifted, bringing chaos to Brightside and Shadowside. And Jesmet, the music mentor who was executed for saving their lives, is alive and promises them a special power called the Numa—if they'll just wait.

Book 3 coming soon!

Pick up a copy today at your favorite bookstore!

Visit www.zondervan.com/teen

Share Your Thoughts

With the Author: Your comments will be forwarded to
the author when you send them to *zauthor@zondervan.com*.

With Zondervan: Submit your review of this book
by writing to *zreview@zondervan.com*.

Free Online Resources at
www.zondervan.com/hello

 Zondervan AuthorTracker: Be notified whenever your favorite authors publish new books, go on tour, or post an update about what's happening in their lives.

 Daily Bible Verses and Devotions: Enrich your life with daily Bible verses or devotions that help you start every morning focused on God.

 Free Email Publications: Sign up for newsletters on fiction, Christian living, church ministry, parenting, and more.

 Zondervan Bible Search: Find and compare Bible passages in a variety of translations at www.zondervanbiblesearch.com.

 Other Benefits: Register yourself to receive online benefits like coupons and special offers, or to participate in research.

ZONDERVAN®
.com